The Case

of the

Crafty Christmas Crooks

All the Best!

Cindy Vincent

Also by Cindy Vincent

The Case of the Cat Show Princess:
A Buckley and Bogey Cat Detective Caper

The Mystery of the Missing Ming:
A Daisy Diamond Detective Novel

The Case of the Rising Star Ruby:
A Daisy Diamond Detective Novel

Makeover For Murder:
A Kate Bundeen Mystery

Cats Are Part of His Kingdom, Too
33 Daily Devotions to Show God's Love

The Case of the Crafty Christmas Crooks

A Buckley and Bogey Cat Detective Caper

Cindy Vincent

Whodunit Press

Houston   Bozeman

The Case of the Crafty Christmas Crooks

A Buckley and Bogey Cat Detective Caper

Published by Whodunit Press

A Division of Mysteries by Vincent, LLC

For information, please contact:

Whodunit Press

c/o Mysteries by Vincent

Mysteriesbyvincent.com

1-866-WHODUNIT

ISBN: 978-1-932169-73-7

Printed in the United States of America

Dedication

To my husband, Rob, the best Cat Dad ever.

CHAPTER 1

Holy Mackerel! I could hardly believe my eyes. There I was, sitting at the top of the stairs with my best friend and brother, Bogart, or "Bogey" for short. We were peeking out between the spindles of the staircase. That meant we had a perfect view of what was going on just below us. Of course, since we're both cat detectives, we were ready to jump into action at a moment's notice. And believe me, judging from what we saw below, we figured we'd have to spring into action at any second! So we sat in a crouched position, and our keen cat eyes took in every movement.

Though to tell you the truth, I guess I was really the only one in a crouched position. And well, I was probably the only one whose eyes were watching every movement. Actually, Bogey was kind of lolling on his side with his eyes closed. He opened them just enough to help himself to a cat treat from a foil pouch. He passed one to me and then closed his eyes again.

But I, Buckley Bergdorf, was almost too nervous to eat the fish-flavored treat. My heart was racing, and I'm sure my long, black fur was standing on end.

I couldn't believe that Bogey wasn't even the least bit worried. Then again, he was a professional when it came to being a cat detective. He'd been in the business for years, ever since he'd been adopted from the cat shelter. As for me, I was barely more than a rookie. In fact, I'd really only solved a few cases so far. Thankfully, I had Bogey to lean on to help me learn the job. He'd been teaching me everything he knew about the cat detective business.

And believe me, there was a lot to learn! But I was happy to have the job and happy to help out my family. Especially since I didn't even have a family for a while.

I still remember the day when my human Mom adopted me and brought me home from the cat shelter. Bogey took me under his paw right away, and I've been grateful for it ever since. After all, I'd once been out on the mean streets with nothing to eat. Now I have a home with plenty of food, and people and cats who love me. Plus I have the best big brother in the world.

I jumped when a loud *whump* suddenly echoed up to us. I noticed yet another box had appeared in the hallway below.

I gulped. "Aren't you scared?" I asked Bogey.

He grabbed another cat treat. "Nope, kid. I've seen this kind of thing before. It happens every year."

I'm sure my eyes went as wide as my food dish. Did he say every year? How could he be so calm when this happened every year? I tried to scratch my head, but I only ended up poking myself in the eye with my huge paw.

Sometimes I was amazed at how different Bogey and I were. Sure, we're both black cats with gold eyes. But he is sleek and slim. His fur is so shiny it looks like patent leather.

As for me, well, I'm a Maine Coon cat. In case you didn't know it, Maine Coon cats are very, very large. And I do mean large! I'm barely two years old and I'm already bigger than some dogs! On top of that, my long, thick fur has three layers, which makes me look even more gigantic. Plus my paws are huge, and I wonder if I'll ever really grow into them. Sometimes it seems like they just get in the way.

And having your paws get in the way isn't good when it comes to being a cat detective. So I work extra hard to make my paws go where I want them to go, when I want them to go there.

I glanced over at Bogey. He never had any problems getting his paws to go in the right direction. He looked like he was half-asleep, but I knew he could be fully alert and ready to go in a half a second if he needed to. In fact, Bogey could run so fast that sometimes his feet barely touched the ground. The other cats in our house said Bogey could even fly. And though I'd never seen it, I believed it was true.

I peeked downstairs again and watched my human Mom drag in still another big box. It made a loud sliding noise across the hardwood floor. She paused and tucked her long, dark hair behind her ears before going on.

Our human sister, Gracie, laughed and flitted from box to box. As she went, she unwrapped all kinds of small objects that she pulled from the big packing boxes. Most of those objects were round and shiny, with strings attached to the top. It seemed like Gracie got more excited with each new thing she unwrapped. Her dark eyes practically danced while she worked.

Gracie is the twelve-year-old daughter of our human Mom and Dad. We love her like she's our real sister, since she's so nice to all the cats who live in our house.

Our human Mom is really sweet to us, too. And we couldn't be happier that she adopted us.

But now I wondered if there was something wrong with our Mom, because what she was doing below us sure seemed strange. And different.

As far as I was concerned, anything strange and different only added up to one thing — something scary!

I scooted a little closer to the staircase railing to get a better look. That's when I noticed my Mom had unpacked a bunch of things that looked like branches from an evergreen tree. And it looked like she was putting something together.

In fact, it looked like our Mom was building . . .

"A tree," I said to Bogey. "Is that a tree?"

But how could that be? And why in the world would she do something like that?

Bogey opened one eye and glanced at the scene downstairs. "Yup, kid. It's a tree."

Holy Catnip! Suddenly I felt like the room was starting to spin.

"Is our Mom okay?" I asked Bogey. "Is she sick? What in the world is going on here?"

Bogey handed me a cat treat. "Here you go, kid. This'll calm your nerves."

I took the treat with shaking paws. "Should we investigate this?" I asked him.

After all, we had opened up the Buckley and Bogey Cat Detective Agency not too long ago.

Bogey grinned at me. "Don't sweat it, kid. We don't need to investigate. They're just getting ready for Christmas."

I munched on the treat. "Christmas? What is Christmas?"

Bogey raised an eyebrow. "You've never had Christmas before? Well, kid, it's kind of a birthday party. A really big birthday party. The biggest."

My mouth dropped open. "Really? I like birthday parties."

When I was at the cat shelter, the volunteers were always having birthday parties. I thought they were fun.

Bogey grinned again. "Well, kid, you're gonna love this one. Christmas is the best. Just you wait and see."

Suddenly I wasn't feeling so nervous anymore. All this for a birthday party? But I'd never seen anyone put up a tree for a party before.

Bogey got up and stretched. "C'mon, kid. Let's go check this out."

I followed Bogey as he ran down the stairs and stopped in front of the new tree. Gazing up at it from the floor, the tree looked like it was really, really tall. But it wasn't exactly like the trees I'd seen outside. And up until now, I guess I'd never realized someone could put a tree together.

Gracie spotted us and squealed. "Look, Buckley! Isn't it going to be pretty? Have you ever seen a Christmas tree before? I'm going to hang all these ornaments on the branches."

She picked me up and held me tight. Then she dipped me over the table so I could see the bunches of ornaments she was talking about. They were in every shape and color a cat could imagine. Some were gold and some were silver. There were green ones and red ones and purple ones. There were cat ornaments and angel ornaments and ornaments in the shape of boats and cars and teddy bears. Some looked very old and some looked brand new.

Yet even though the ornaments were all different, they were all really, really shiny. Some even sparkled.

"Isn't it wonderful, Buckley? Isn't this great?" Gracie squealed. Her dark eyes glowed and she held me close again. Then she began to dance and spin around the room. She went around and around and around, with her long dark hair flying out behind her.

I hung on for dear life. For some reason, Gracie seemed to be going through a "spinning phase" lately. I only hoped she would grow out of it soon. Right now would have been nice, since it seemed like she kept on spinning and spinning forever. I couldn't believe how much one little girl could spin. She finally stopped, but for some reason, it still felt like the room was going around in circles.

Gracie put me down and I stumbled kind of zig-zaggity toward the tree. Then I stopped and blinked a few times, trying to get my bearings again. Just as I did, a lean, long-haired white cat came racing down the hallway. She was headed right for us. At top speed. I thought she would put on the brakes when she saw the tree. But no! She just zoomed even faster.

The next thing I knew, she went straight up that tree.

It was the Princess.

Or Lexie, as the humans in our house called her most of the time. She was the newest cat to join our family. She had once been a show cat who was expected to be prim and perfect. But now that she lived with us, well, she'd changed a little. Now she acted a lot more free and she usually raced around the house at lightning speed.

She meowed with delight and gazed down at me with her big, green eyes.

And let me tell you, those green eyes made me a whole lot dizzier than spinning with Gracie had.

Holy Mackerel.

My Mom tried to reach up into the tree to get the Princess down. But the Princess had other ideas. I guess she must have liked the view from the top of that tree.

Gracie laughed while my Mom tried to coax the Princess down.

Then the Princess leaned to the right, and suddenly the tree started to lean with her. So she tried to stop it by leaning to the left. But the tree went left, too. That's when the Princess leaned back to the right, then to the left again, and before we knew it, the whole tree was swaying. Back and forth. Back and forth. Back and forth.

I felt my fur stand on end while my jaw practically hit the floor. Beside me, Bogey just rolled his eyes.

Now the Princess dug in with her claws and held on for all she was worth.

But it was too late.

The tree started to tip farther and farther and farther to the left. Seconds later, it came crashing down to the ground! Branches landed everywhere and the Princess went flying off. She zoomed like a streak down the hallway until she disappeared.

Holy Catnip!

Bogey shook his head. "Dames," he said. "I never could make heads nor tails of 'em."

Gracie giggled and giggled and couldn't stop.

My Mom just sighed. "I guess we'll have to get out the heavy-duty tree stand," she said to Gracie. "Otherwise little Lexie will tip this over again. Could you please get it from the attic for me?"

Gracie nodded, even though she couldn't stop giggling. She was still laughing when she ran up the stairs.

I had just tiptoed over to take a good look at the fallen tree when the doorbell rang.

This brought Bogey and me to attention right away. That's because part of our jobs as cat detectives is to watch over the security of our home. We run surveillance on our house every night, and sometimes several times a night. And if you don't know what the word surveillance means, well, it's just a fancy word that means checking things out to make sure everything is okay. You know, so we can make sure our family is safe and sound.

My Mom walked over to the door, looked through the peephole, and smiled. She opened the door and a rush of chilly air ruffled my fur. After all, the days had been getting shorter and the nights were getting a whole lot cooler.

Officer Phoebe Smiley of the St. Gertrude Police Department stood on our front porch. We had worked with Officer Smiley on another case. Though like most humans, she really had no idea that we were actually the ones who had solved the case.

Probably because cats always switch to cat language whenever humans are around. Plus, some humans have no clue what cats are capable of.

Our Mom opened the door wider to let her in. "Hello, Phoebe. So nice to see you again."

Officer Smiley stepped inside and pulled out her notebook. "Nice to see you, too, Abby. But I wish I was here under better circumstances."

Bogey and I glanced at each other and then tilted our ears forward.

Our Mom's eyebrows went up. "Oh? What's happened?"

Officer Smiley shook her head. "The Christmas season has barely even begun and we've already had our first break-in."

My Mom put her hand to her chest. "Oh no! Where? Did they take anything valuable?"

Officer Smiley sighed. "I'm afraid so. It happened to the Mitchells, your neighbors down the street. They decided to do their Christmas shopping early this year. They already had their tree up and all the presents wrapped and put underneath."

Okay, let me tell you, that's when my ears really perked up. Did Officer Smiley just say "presents"? Were presents going under our tree, too?

I glanced back at our tree, which was still lying on the ground in pieces. Wow, this was going to be some birthday party. Must be for someone very, very special.

I turned back to Officer Smiley.

She flipped a page in her notebook. "A crook — or — crooks broke into their house while they were out to the movies last night, which was Saturday night, of course. The crooks took everything. All the presents. They stole the wreath right off the front door, too. Mrs. Mitchell reports that they even took some of the Christmas cookies she'd made. Though oddly enough, they only stole the cookies shaped like stars. They left all the other shapes alone."

My Mom's dark eyes went wide. "That's so awful! I'll be sure to start a collection for the Mitchells at my antique store. We'll see if we can't raise enough money to buy more presents for them."

Officer Smiley nodded her head and moved her pen in position to take notes. "That would be wonderful, Abigail. In the meantime, have you or your family seen anything suspicious around the neighborhood?"

My Mom shook her head. "No, we haven't seen a thing. But we'll be sure to call you if we do see something."

That's when I saw Bogey twitch his tail. It always made him mad when the police didn't bother to find out what the cats might have seen. Cats, after all, are better observers than most humans.

Officer Smiley flipped her notebook closed. "Christmas crooks are especially mean-hearted. And if we don't catch them, they could ruin Christmas for everyone."

Ruin Christmas? I could hardly believe my ears. I had barely even learned about Christmas and how great it was. And now I was already hearing that someone might ruin it for me, too. All in one short hour.

What else might happen?

Holy Mackerel!

CHAPTER 2

Shortly after Officer Smiley left, Bogey and I planted ourselves in the dining room, right off the front hallway and not too far from the front door. Our Mom went back to putting the tree together, and Bogey immediately turned to stare out the window. His eyes darted to every leaf and blade of grass that moved outside.

Holy Catnip! He sure seemed serious about looking out the window. He was obviously back on the job as a cat detective. And if he was looking out the window, I figured I'd better look out the window, too.

Though to tell you the truth, I wasn't really sure what we were looking for.

I glanced at my brother. "Um . . . Bogey . . . is there anything special we should watch for?"

"Yup, kid," Bogey said without averting his gaze. "Keep your eyes peeled for anything that seems out of place. Or anyone."

I swallowed hard. "What do you mean, 'out of place'?"

Bogey nodded at the window. "Someone or something that doesn't belong. Someone who doesn't fit somehow."

I looked outside just as hard as I could. "Um, okay."

I saw trees and grass and birds flying by. I saw neighbor kids playing and grown-ups out walking their dogs.

"Is there any reason we're doing this?" I asked Bogey.

He turned to me. "Yup, kid. You heard what the officer said. We've got a burglar on the loose. Someone who wants to break into houses and steal stuff. Our family would be pretty shook up if someone broke in here."

Boy, he sure had that right! If a burglar showed up at our house, I knew I'd be pretty scared. Terrified, even. And sometimes when I got really scared I forgot everything I'd learned about being a cat detective. The things that Bogey had taught me went right out the window. And I don't mean the front window, either.

The problem was, cat detectives were supposed to be brave and fearless. Like Bogey. Unfortunately, I was still working on the brave and fearless part. And so far, it wasn't exactly going well.

"I'll do my very best," I promised him.

He touched his forehead like he was tipping a hat. "I knew I could count on you, kid. With a burglar running around out there, we've gotta run a tight ship. Burglars don't usually stop with just one house. Once they get a taste for crime, they usually develop an appetite for more. So we've gotta run surveillance every few hours and step up on security."

"Aye, aye," I said. I tried to salute him but I only ended up poking myself in the nose with my huge paw. "Is there anything else we can do?"

Bogey sat up straight and tall. "Yup, kid. Our best bet is to solve this case. We need to catch this burglar and send them up the river."

I gulped. "Up the river?"

Bogey put his paw on my shoulder. "To jail, kid. Jail."

"Wow," I breathed. "You mean the Buckley and Bogey Cat Detective Agency has a new case?"

Bogey turned an ear in my direction. "You got it, kid. And we're the clients. Or maybe I should say, our family is. Only, they don't know it."

Right about then, I'm sure my eyes went really, really wide. Holy Catnip! A new case? I sat up nice and tall just like Bogey did. If we had a case to solve, that meant I had to work extra hard and be the best cat detective I could be.

I glanced into the hallway at our Mom for a second. "So where do we start?"

Bogey shook his head. "That's a tough one, kid. We really need to see the scene of the crime. It'll give us a better picture of what happened. We've gotta get over to the Mitchells' house somehow."

Bogey was right. That was a tough one. Especially since the cats in our house were all housecats. We weren't exactly supposed to go outside.

Now Gracie skipped into the hallway and joined our Mom again. She brought the extra heavy-duty tree stand with her. Then she helped our Mom put the main pole of the tree into the stand. Thankfully, this stand looked like it was really strong, and I was pretty sure the tree wouldn't tip over again.

Not even if the Princess ran straight up the tree and danced the Hokey Pokey.

I turned back to Bogey. "But how will we get to the Mitchells'?"

Bogey rubbed his whiskers. "I don't know yet, kid. I'm working on it. I'll let you know just as soon as I figure it out. But be ready in case we have to move fast."

"I'll be ready," I said. Though to tell you the truth, I wasn't really sure if I would ever be ready.

Behind us, our Mom told Gracie about the burglary while they finished attaching the last branches to the Christmas tree.

Gracie gasped. "Oh no! That's so sad. To have somebody steal all the Christmas presents!"

My ears perked up again. That was the second time I'd heard someone mention presents. And boy did I like presents! Then again, what cat didn't love a nice present every now and then? Clearly, it was high time I investigated and found out more about these presents. But only so that I could be a good cat detective, of course. And because it might help me solve the case.

I turned back to Bogey. "Why does everyone keep talking about presents? Are there presents at Christmas?"

Bogey grabbed a bag of cat treats he kept hidden behind a potted palm. "Yup, kid. There are presents, all right. Lots of 'em. For everybody. They're all wrapped up in bright paper and put under the tree. Then everybody opens their presents on Christmas morning."

Wow, this Christmas thing was sounding better and better.

"But where do the presents come from?" I asked him.

He grabbed a treat from the bag and passed the bag to me. "Lots of places, kid. Some from our Mom and Dad and Gracie. Others come from friends. And some of them come from Santa Claus."

I used a claw to pull a treat out of the bag. "Santa Claus? Who is Santa Claus?"

Bogey polished off his first treat and took another. "He's a big guy. Dressed in a red fuzzy suit. He's got a long white beard and he comes down the chimney. But he only brings presents to good boys and girls. And good cats, too. I'm guessing he might even bring presents to good dogs. But that one I don't know for sure."

By now I felt like the room was spinning again. "He comes down the chimney? Why does he do that?"

Bogey inched closer to the window. "It's quicker, kid. He rides through the sky in a sleigh pulled by flying reindeer. Then he comes down the chimney and drops off the presents and takes off again."

I blinked hard a few times. "Wow. He must be some guy."

Bogey nodded. "You got it, kid. He is. Us cats have met Santa a time or two. The people never see him though. They're always in bed."

I tried to rub my forehead with my paw. But I only ended up poking myself in the ear. "Amazing. I sure hope I get to see him."

Bogey grinned at me. "Maybe you will, kid. Maybe you will. He'll be here on Christmas Eve. Late. Very late."

Now it was my turn to grin. Bogey and I were always up late at night since that's when we ran surveillance on our house. That meant I would be awake when Santa showed up. And after what Bogey had told me, I really wanted to meet this guy.

I heard a strange *brrrrrp, rrrrrrp* kind of noise behind me. I looked back to see our Mom and Gracie pulling lots and lots of green strands from another big box. Each of those strands had tiny colored lights attached from one end to the other.

Holy Mackerel!

Now what were they doing? Was this more stuff for Christmas? I closed my eyes for a moment. I'd seen and learned so many new things in one short afternoon that I could hardly believe it. It was almost more than a two-year-old cat could take.

I felt Bogey touch my paw and hand me another treat. "Don't sweat it, kid. Those are just the lights. They put lights all over that tree to make it sparkle and shine."

This time I just took the treat without saying a word. I wondered how much more new stuff I was going to learn today.

Before long, our Mom and Gracie had those lights wrapped around and around the tree. They plugged the strands in and suddenly the whole thing lit up. There were white lights and green lights and red lights. There were blue lights and yellow lights and pink lights. Some lights flashed on and off. And some danced up and down the strands.

Gracie stepped back to admire it, and I just sat there with my mouth hanging open.

She knelt down to pet me. "Isn't it pretty, Buckley?"

Boy, she sure had that right. "Pretty" was the word. I stood up and gave her a little rub with my head.

All the while I couldn't take my eyes off that tree. The colors kept flashing before my eyes, and I couldn't stop watching them. When I finally did look away, I kept on seeing colors and lights flashing.

I could barely make out Bogey sitting in front of the window.

He grinned. "Seeing spots, kid? Happens if you stare at those lights too long. Rookie mistake. But they'll go away."

I sure hoped so.

Our Mom placed a big, shiny star on the top of the tree. Then she and Gracie started to hang the ornaments on the branches. I could hardly believe all the stuff they were going to put on that one big tree. Before long, we wouldn't even be able to see the branches anymore.

Gracie pulled a plastic ornament from the bunch and knelt down next to me. "See, Buckley? This ornament is for the cats in the family. We'll put a few on the bottom just for you."

Holy Catnip! The cats in our house even got their own ornaments?

I leaned in to take a good look at the ornament. It was a figure of a big guy in a red suit with a long white beard. He had a sack of presents slung over his shoulder.

Right about then, I think my eyes were about to pop out of my head. "Bogey . . . is this . . . is this . . .?"

Bogey didn't even wait for me to finish. "That's the guy, kid. That's Santa."

I followed Gracie over to the tree. Seconds later, she had the ornament hanging from one of the lowest branches. I sat up tall so I was almost eye level with this little Santa. I'd never had my own ornament before. I vowed to look at it every single day.

Our Mom and Gracie had just finished decorating the tree when the kitchen oven timer went off. I could smell the casserole our Mom had cooking in the oven.

"Good thing I made two," our Mom said to Gracie. "Let's take one down to the Mitchells to cheer them up. We'll be back before your Dad finishes up in his woodshop."

"Good idea, Mom," Gracie told her. "I'll get our coats."

I smiled over at Bogey. Our Mom was famous for doing nice things for people. And cats. She did nice things for us every day.

Bogey suddenly jumped to his feet. "This is it, kid!"

I looked around the room. "It is? What is?"

Bogey raced to the front door. "This is our chance, kid. This is how we'll see the scene of the crime. We're going to the Mitchells' house."

For a moment I wondered if Bogey had been hitting the cat treats a little too hard. "We are?"

Bogey grinned. "You got it, kid. Just follow my lead."

Minutes later, our Mom had one of the casseroles wrapped up in a bag with handles. She and Gracie both put on their coats, and they were almost ready to go.

That's when Bogey meowed and waved at me. "C'mon, kid. Time to be as cute as you can be."

"Huh . . . what?" I barely managed to squeak out before Bogey stretched up my Mom's leg.

Our Mom laughed. "Do you want to go with us, Bogey? Okay, you can come. I can't think of anyone who could cheer someone up better than you could."

She picked up Bogey and he stretched up to her shoulder. She carried the casserole bag with her other hand.

"Hurry, kid," Bogey hollered to me.

"Hurry?" For the life of me, I couldn't figure out what Bogey wanted me to do.

Bogey nodded toward Gracie. "Get Gracie to bring you. Put up a real fuss if you have to."

I blinked hard. "Oh, okay."

Then I raced over to Gracie and began to rub around her legs. She petted me, but she just kept on fastening her coat.

"Don't worry, Buckley," she said. "We'll bring Bogey back soon."

Did she say she'd bring Bogey back soon? That sounded like she didn't plan to take me, too!

So I moved around her legs even faster. I kept meowing and purring as loud as I could.

She giggled and stepped forward. "Oh, Buckley. I love you, too. I'll see you in a little bit."

"C'mon, kid!" Bogey meowed. "You can do this! Get into her arms. You've gotta come see this crime scene, too!"

Suddenly my heart started to pound really loud inside my chest. I knew I had to convince Gracie to take me. But how?

Then I remembered a trick I'd learned from Lil Bits, another cat who lived in our house. Lil had been a cat detective for years. And after retiring from the job for a while, she had recently decided to come back.

Before then, she'd taught me everything she knew about looking cute.

So I jumped in front of the door, stood up on my hind legs and tilted my head to the side. I looked right at Gracie and meowed.

Gracie laughed and rolled her eyes. "Oh, Buckley, you are the cutest cat ever."

Then she knelt down to pet me.

Just as soon as she did, I gave her a big wet kiss on the nose. While she was still giggling, I jumped into her arms and dug my claws firmly into her wool coat. I hung on so tight it would have taken a pry bar to pull me off.

She hugged me close. "Okay, Buckley. You win. You can come with us."

Across from me, Bogey leaned over our Mom's shoulder. He gave me a "paws up." "Way to go, kid."

And to tell you the truth, I was kind of proud of myself. But I figured I'd better not get too smug. After all, we hadn't even gotten to the scene of the crime yet. For all I knew, that could be one big, scary adventure just waiting to happen.

Gracie opened the door and we all went outside. A cold wind suddenly whipped around us. I was pretty sure I even saw a snowflake or two fly by.

I snuggled in tight against Gracie. That's when I wondered if going to the Mitchells' house to see the crime scene was such a good idea.

Who knew what we might find?

Holy Mackerel!

CHAPTER 3

Holy Mackerel! Snowflakes started to fly all around us as our Mom and Gracie carried Bogey and me down the street. A few of the wet flakes landed on my face and my ears. I tried to wipe them off with my huge paw but I nearly poked myself in the eye. So I just tucked my head under Gracie's chin instead. Funny, but even though it was chilly outside, I really wasn't too cold. Probably thanks to the extra layers in my fur coat. Maine Coon cats are geared for cold weather and snow. After all, my cat ancestors came from Maine, a state that has lots of harsh winters. Our fur coats keep us warm and our big paws make it easier for us to run through snow.

Even so, it was still nice to cuddle up with Gracie. A cat can never get too much cuddling.

Especially since I was already kind of nervous about going to investigate a crime scene. Because, to tell you the truth, I hadn't exactly investigated very many crime scenes.

Bogey, on the other hand, had investigated lots of crime scenes. He was an expert and knew exactly what to do.

I peeked around Gracie's shoulder to see how he was holding up in the chilly weather. I noticed he was shivering a little while our Mom carried him. That was the problem with being such a lean cat like Bogey. Even though his size made him lightning fast, he didn't have enough fat or fur to keep him warm.

We arrived at the Mitchells' house just a few minutes later. The Mitchells lived at the end of our block, five doors down from us. Their house was a really old place, kind of like ours. But their house had a huge porch that wrapped all the way around the front and sides.

Gracie carried me up the rickety old steps, and I held on tight. I could hardly believe I was about to set paw inside the very place where someone had committed a crime. Holy Catnip! And so close to our own house, too. The idea of it made me start to shake just a little bit myself.

My Mom rang the doorbell, and then we waited for someone to answer the door. When no one answered, we waited and waited some more. But still no one came to the door. So she rang the bell again.

Finally, we heard some shuffling inside the house. A few seconds later, the door opened just a crack.

"Yes?" said a woman's voice.

"Hello, Mesmeralda," our Mom said with a cheerful voice. "It's us, your neighbors from down the street. Abigail and Gracie Abernathy."

Mrs. Mitchell opened the door a little wider. "Oh, hello. What do you want?"

Our Mom nodded at her. "We just heard what happened. And we wanted to tell you how sorry we were to hear you'd been robbed."

Gracie smiled up at her. "And we brought you a casserole for dinner."

Mrs. Mitchell shook her head, and her straight, brown hair flopped on her forehead. "You sure didn't need to do that. But it's very thoughtful of you."

"Not a problem," our Mom assured her. "I made one for us as well. Would you please open the door so I can hand this to you? We won't come in and bother you if you're busy."

That's when I saw Bogey glance in my direction. "This isn't looking good, kid," he meowed. "If she doesn't let us in, we'll never get to that crime scene."

Holy Mackerel! Bogey was right. It would be pretty bad if we came all this way in the cold and didn't get to investigate!

Mrs. Mitchell frowned and pulled the door open a few more inches. "Well, this isn't the best time. I am rather busy at the moment."

"Okay, kid," Bogey meowed back to me. "It's now or never. I'm going in!"

What? Did Bogey just say he was going in? But how? Mrs. Mitchell clearly wasn't about to welcome us inside her house. In fact, she didn't seem like she wanted visitors at all. Maybe that's what happens to people after someone breaks into their home.

She sighed and reached out to take the casserole from our Mom.

Just as she did, Bogey made his move.

In one quick, black streak, he dove between Mrs. Mitchell's legs and landed inside the entryway. Then he pushed off with his back legs and went racing down the hall.

I could hardly believe it! Mrs. Mitchell gasped and Gracie squealed. And I'm sure my eyes went as wide as the casserole dish.

"Bogey," Gracie hollered. "Bogey! Come back here."

But he was out of sight.

Mrs. Mitchell squinted at me with gray eyes. "You brought your cats with you?"

Gracie held me up so my face was just a few inches from Mrs. Mitchell's. "We thought they might cheer you up."

I tried to look as adorable as I could, while Mrs.
Mitchell just stared at me.

"I'm so sorry, Mesmeralda," my Mom said. "Bogey's
usually a perfect gentleman. I don't know what's gotten
into him."

Mrs. Mitchell sighed. "Well, I guess you'll have to
come in and catch him, then."

With those words, she opened the door for all of us.
Then she led us to the kitchen without saying anything.
Gracie put me on a stool in front of the counter while
she went to look for Bogey.

The aroma of cookies baking filled the air in the
comfy, warm kitchen. The countertop was covered with
bowls and cookie sheets and cookie cutters. So I
guessed Mrs. Mitchell really had been busy.

My Mom touched Mrs. Mitchell's arm. "I know this
must be upsetting for you, Mesmeralda. I can't even
begin to imagine what you must be going through."

Mrs. Mitchell sighed. "Yes, Abigail, it has been very
upsetting for us. We'd spent all the money we could on
those Christmas presents. We did our shopping early so
we could relax and enjoy Christmas. Now I don't know
what we'll do."

My Mom reached over and gave her a hug. "Don't
worry, Mesmeralda. St. Gertrude is a tight-knit
community. Everyone will pull together to help."

Mrs. Mitchell started to scoop cookies from a cookie
sheet. I'd never seen so many cookies in so many
shapes before in my whole life. There were cookies
shaped like Christmas trees and Christmas ornaments.
There were angels and bells and one that looked a lot
like my Santa Claus ornament. Plus there were holly
leaves and snowflakes and candy canes.

On another plate, I saw cookies in those same
shapes that had been decorated with icing in all
different colors. There were cookies with red icing, green
icing, white icing and blue icing. Some of them even
had sprinkles on top of them.

Holy Catnip!   Each cookie was so pretty, it was almost like a work of art.

If only there had been tuna-flavored cookies, too.

I glanced around the counter, just in case there might be some fish-shaped cookies.

But instead I spotted a sales receipt from Nunzio's Novelties and Knick-Knacks Shop.   That was the store right next to my Mom's antique store!   I'd even met Nunzio, the owner, a few times, when our Mom took us to work with her.   Though I had to say, I always got a funny feeling around him.   He would smile with his mouth, but his black eyes always looked really, really mad.   He would look at us cats, but never, ever pet us.   Bogey said the guy made his fur stand on end.   And let me tell you, cats are pretty good when it comes to seeing a human's real character.

I glanced at the receipt again, and suddenly I remembered something Bogey had taught me.   When he trained me to be a cat detective, he told me I should always be observant.   That meant I was supposed to take a close look at everything around me.   I was supposed to notice the people and the animals and all the things nearby.   He even told me to pretend I was taking a snapshot of all those things.   Then I was supposed to put those things in my memory.   Just in case I might need to remember them again later on.

So now I had to wonder, was this one of those times when I should be really observant?   Was it possible I had found some important clue?   After all, it seemed like the hero in detective shows always found a sales receipt that led them to the criminal.   Wouldn't it be wonderful if I had uncovered a big clue that led us to crack this case?

Holy Mackerel!

All of a sudden, I started to get excited.   I glanced around to make sure no one was watching me.   When I saw the coast was clear, I scooted closer to take a better look at the receipt.   Could this be something the burglar had left behind? Maybe a receipt for buying break-in tools? With the burglar's name and address printed right at the top?

A smile crossed my face. I could practically hear the praise from Bogey, as I imagined him patting me on the back. "Great job, kid," he would say. "You're becoming a first-rate detective!"

Just thinking about it pushed me to finally move close enough to read the receipt. That's when I let out a sigh. It was nothing but a receipt for cookie cutters. It had Mrs. Mitchell's name and address at the top, and it was dated a week ago. In the lines below that, it said, "Christmas Cookie Cutter set #1" and "Christmas Cookie Cutter set #2." But then it looked like Nunzio had written in at the bottom, "If you don't bring me some cookies, I'll just have to steal some."

Holy Mackerel!

Had I read that receipt right?

I glanced again at my Mom and Mrs. Mitchell. Thankfully, they were still talking and didn't even notice me. So I grabbed the receipt in my mouth. Then I quietly jumped down from the stool and tiptoed out of the kitchen. I needed to show this receipt to Bogey right away.

But first I had to find him. I wondered if he had found the scene of the crime already. Maybe he'd found a few clues himself.

In any case, one thing was for sure, I had to hurry. I had to figure out where he'd gone before anyone realized I was missing. And I had to be as stealthy as I could, so no one would spot me running around the house.

Thanks to Bogey, I knew exactly how to be stealthy. I'd even had some experience being stealthy before. It meant I had to keep low to the ground and move along fast, so no one would notice me. Not exactly an easy thing for a big guy like me to do.

Still, I slinked from room to room. First past the dining room, and then into the living room. There I found Gracie, trying to coax Bogey out from behind a huge Christmas tree. The tree was tucked into the corner, and Bogey was busy sniffing the ground.

Gracie kneeled on the floor and turned to me. "Oh good, Buckley. Can you get Bogey to come out?"

I rubbed up against Gracie and dropped the receipt into her coat pocket.

Then I meowed to my brother. "Have you found anything?"

He nodded to me. "Yup, kid. I found plenty."

Right about then, my chin practically fell to the floor. "You did? What did you find?"

I glanced from the bottom of the tree all the way up to the huge, gold star on the top. I sure didn't see any clues or anything important for this case.

Bogey called out from behind the tree. "Nothing. Absolutely nothing."

I blinked a couple of times and shook my head.

Wait a minute. First he told me he found plenty, and then he told me he found nothing. What in the world was going on?

Holy Catnip!

CHAPTER 4

Holy Mackerel! I took a look at my brother and wondered if he was okay. Because one thing was for sure — he wasn't making any sense. Maybe Bogey had been overdoing it with the cat treats.

He sniffed the bottom branch of the tree and squinted his eyes. "Amazing," he said.

It was? I padded across the bare, wooden floor and joined him behind the Christmas tree.

"What is amazing?" I asked him. "And how you can find 'nothing' and 'plenty' at the same time?"

Bogey grinned at me. "It's easy, kid. I'll show you. First, take a sniff of that branch."

I did as he said. In fact, I took a really good sniff. And another one, just to be sure.

Let me tell you, cats have a really good sense of smell. And when I say really good, well, I mean *really* good. In fact, a cat's sense of smell is about fourteen times better than a human's. With one sniff, I can tell if any people or cats have been in the area. Plus I can pick up lots and lots of other scents as well. Sometimes these are smells that have been there for a while. And sometimes these are smells that have been brought in from somewhere else, either by humans or animals.

For instance, if a person walked in from a flower garden, believe me, a cat would know it. Because that person would bring the scent of flowers in with them, and a cat could smell it.

Bogey turned to me. "So what did you pick up, kid?"

"Well . . ." I started slowly. "It just smells like the rest of the house. And like Mrs. Mitchell. And maybe a man's scent, too."

"You got it, kid. That man's scent is all over the house. So I'm guessing it belongs to Mr. Mitchell."

I tilted my ears forward, so I could listen better. "Uh-huh. That makes sense."

Bogey touched the branch with his paw. "Do you smell any other people on the branch or in this corner?"

I shook my head. "Nope." Then I hesitated a minute. "Well, I think I might smell a little bit of Officer Phoebe Smiley. But no one else."

Bogey nodded and glanced at the floor. "Okay, kid, now take a look around. Do you see anything out of place? Or any disturbance in the dust? Do you see any bits or clues left behind?"

I did as Bogey told me. I looked around twice and couldn't find a thing except for our paw prints. Not a single clue. And not a single thing out of place.

I turned to my brother. "I don't see anything."

Bogey grinned at me. "Not a thing. In other words, nothing, right?"

I nodded. "Right."

Bogey leaned back and looked up into the tree. "So in finding absolutely nothing, we have learned plenty."

I crinkled my brow. "We have?"

Bogey stood on his hind legs and reached a little higher into the tree. "That's right, kid. We have learned that the burglar was a real mastermind. A criminal mastermind."

Right about then, I'm sure my eyes went really wide.
"They were? How can you tell?"

He returned to the floor. "Because, kid, they broke
into this house, and stole all the Christmas presents
and some other things. Then they vanished and didn't
leave a single trace behind. Not even so much as a
scent. Only a criminal mastermind could do that."

"Wow," I whispered.

I could hardly believe my ears. A criminal
mastermind. Why did the crook have to be a criminal
mastermind? Why couldn't we have come across a
crook who wasn't too bright? Or, as Lil Bits would say,
a cat who was a few fish short of a whole can of tuna?

I tried to cover my eyes with my paw, but I only
ended up poking myself in the ear.

"Have you ever seen anything like this before?" I
asked Bogey.

He shook his head. "Nope, kid. Not in all my years
of being a cat detective. This might be our toughest case
ever."

Holy Catnip! Did he say the toughest case ever? I
was really hoping to get a few more of the easy cases
under my belt first. Like the time I solved the Mystery of
the Missing Cat Toys. Turns out the Princess had
stored them all in a closet and forgot to tell us. Then
there was the Mystery of the Missing Cat Treats. I
solved that right away when I learned Gracie had
accidentally put them on the wrong shelf in the pantry.
If only I could have practiced on a few more cases like
those. Before I started in on the really tough cases.

Gracie called to us from the other side of the tree
again. "Please, please, please, Buckley and Bogey.
Please come out. If you don't come out, I won't ever be
allowed to take you to someone's house again."

With those words, Bogey nodded toward Gracie.
"Time to go, kid. Besides, we've learned all we needed to
know here."

He trotted out to Gracie and I followed him. Then we each climbed into one of Gracie's arms and let her pick us up.

"Thank you, boys," she said as she hugged us tight. She kissed Bogey and then me on the head. "You two have got to stop running off when we go somewhere."

Seconds later, she had us back in the kitchen. Our Mom and Mrs. Mitchell were still talking, and they were looking at some big, donut-shaped objects on the table. Those objects appeared to be made from pine tree branches. They had bows and ornaments and all kinds of decorations attached to them.

"What are those?" I meowed to Bogey.

"Christmas wreaths, kid," he meowed back. "People hang 'em on their front doors at Christmastime."

Holy Mackerel. This whole Christmas thing was just getting bigger and bigger. I couldn't believe all the stuff I'd learned about Christmas in one short afternoon. Now I wondered what else there was to know about this holiday.

Our Mom pointed to one of the wreaths. "This one is especially beautiful," she said. "I like the way it's tied with a big, red velvet bow. And I love all the little shiny ball ornaments attached."

"Thank you," Mrs. Mitchell replied. "Did I tell you they're for sale? Would you like to buy one?"

Our Mom blinked once or twice. Then she smiled and said, "Well, certainly. I'd be happy to." She pulled some money from her pocket and paid Mrs. Mitchell.

It looked like we were going to have a Christmas wreath on our door, too.

Our Mom picked up the wreath she'd just bought. "You know," she said, "the St. Gertrude Citywide Charity is hosting a gigantic craft fair at the St Gertrude Events Center this Saturday. People will be selling all kinds of homemade items. Maybe you'd like to sell your wreaths there, too."

"Yes," Gracie chimed in. "I'm going to be selling cat Christmas collars that I made."

Oh, boy. Did she say cat Christmas collars? Did that mean cats wore special collars for Christmas? My head was starting to spin with all the things I'd learned about Christmas.

For the first time since we'd arrived, Mrs. Mitchell smiled. "Why, I'd love to sell my wreaths at the Craft Fair. I'll make up a whole bunch of them!"

Our Mom smiled back. "Great! I'll make sure they reserve a booth for you. I'm sure you'll sell tons. And it'll help you make some money to replace all the Christmas presents that were stolen."

Mrs. Mitchell didn't say a word, but merely nodded.

"And don't worry," our Mom added. "The people of St. Gertrude are very generous. I'm sure everyone will chip in to help you out since you've been robbed."

Mrs. Mitchell smiled again. But this time, her eyes weren't smiling along with her mouth. "That's very kind of you, Abigail. But I don't want to be a bother. My husband and I really don't want any special attention."

Our Mom nodded. "I understand, Mesmeralda. I understand."

Minutes later, we were walking back to our house again. By now it had gotten dark outside and the streetlamps shined from above. Snow still swirled around us while our Mom carried Bogey and the new wreath. I cuddled in with Gracie so the snowflakes would stay off my face.

All the while I couldn't stop thinking about what Bogey had said earlier. Whoever had broken into the Mitchells' house was a criminal mastermind. A criminal mastermind who had been only five doors down from us.

Was it possible this same crook might try to go after our house, too?

I peeked my head out and glanced around. That's when I noticed the Christmas wreath on the front door of the Nelsons' house. The house next door to the

Mitchells'. I wondered if they'd bought a wreath from Mrs. Mitchell, too. Since it looked a lot like the Christmas wreath we were going to have on our front door.

For some reason, the thought of it made me smile. Especially when I wondered if the rest of the neighbors would have wreaths on their doors.

I looked around the neighborhood again. And then suddenly, I had a creepy feeling that made my fur stand on end. I kind of felt like we were being watched by someone. But when I glanced around once more, I didn't see anyone at all.

I meowed to my brother. "Bogey, I've sort of got this funny feeling that . . ."

I didn't even have a chance to get the words out before he answered me. "Yup, kid. I know what you're going to say. It feels like someone is watching us."

"You feel it, too?" I asked him.

He nodded and kept looking around. "Yup, I do. Take it from me, kid. Always trust your gut instinct. If something doesn't feel right, it probably isn't."

I gulped. "Uh . . . okay."

I started to shake, even though I wasn't cold.

Gracie laughed. "What's wrong, Buckley? You're acting like you're scared or something. Don't worry. We'll be home soon."

Not soon enough, as far as I was concerned.

I had to wonder, why would someone be watching us? And who would be watching us? Could it be the burglars? Were they thinking of breaking into our house next?

I had seen how sad and quiet Mrs. Mitchell had acted. She looked like she was still pretty upset about the break-in and the burglary.

And let me tell you, I sure didn't want my family to be sad or upset. I didn't want our Christmas presents to be stolen. I wanted to do everything I could to make sure the burglars didn't break into our house.

Earlier Bogey had told me we'd have to run extra surveillance at night to keep our family safe. But he'd also said that our best option was to catch this crook and send him to jail. Before he broke into another house. And another house.

But *how* would we catch this crook? Or crooks? Especially when this crook was a criminal mastermind? Bogey said this could be our toughest case ever, and well, he wasn't kidding.

Now the question was, were we smart enough to outsmart this very smart burglar?

Holy Catnip!

CHAPTER 5

Holy Mackerel! That night, while our Mom and Dad and Gracie ate dinner, they talked about the break-in at the Mitchells. In fact, it seemed like that was all they talked about.

Of course, Bogey and I sat on the floor nearby, where we could hear every word.

"Let's make sure we keep the doors and windows locked," our Dad said. "Plus we should keep some lights on whenever we leave the house."

Gracie nodded. "So people will think someone is home, right?"

Our Dad smiled. "Exactly."

"I've read where it's a good idea to leave a pair of boots at the front door," our Mom added. "So it looks like someone just got there and took their boots off."

Gracie smiled. "And it makes it look like that person is still there."

"You're right," our Mom told her. "Would you like to be in charge of putting some boots out front?"

"I'll do it tonight," Gracie said.

After dinner, our Mom went into the office and worked on the computer. Our Dad returned to his woodshop in the garage. Pretty soon I heard kind of a high-pitched buzzing sound.

I tilted my ears away, so the noise wasn't so loud. I'd heard that sound before, and it usually sent me running to hide under a bed. I was just about to run again, but Bogey put his paw up.

"Don't sweat it, kid," he told me. "Nothing to worry about."

"What is that noise?" I asked him.

"It's a power saw, kid. Our Dad makes Christmas lawn ornaments out of wood. Then he paints 'em. He'll be selling them at the Craft Fair."

"He does?" I tried to smack myself in the forehead with my huge paw but I only poked myself in the mouth. "Lawn ornaments? People put out lawn ornaments for Christmas, too?"

Bogey grinned. "Yup, you got it, kid. All part of the fun."

I shook my head and wondered what kind of ornaments people put on their lawns. Before I could ask Bogey, Gracie came into the kitchen. She set her sewing machine on the table and dropped an armful of stuff beside it.

That's when Bogey waved good-bye and took off running. Funny, he didn't run from the sound of our Dad's power saw, but Gracie's sewing project sent him racing from the room.

I wondered why.

But I wasn't about to join Bogey. Because I was just dying to know what Gracie was up to. So I watched while she plugged in her machine and organized a whole bunch of fabric strips. I could see strips in red, white, green, and gold shiny fabrics.

Then I watched while she sewed some of the strips together. But I still couldn't tell what she was making.

So I jumped up on the chair next to her.

Gracie immediately smiled and leaned over to show me what she'd been working on. "See, Buckley? Here's one of the cat Christmas collars that I already made."

She held it closer so I could get a better look. And sure enough, it looked like a collar, all right. Only it was made from a bright red fabric and had little round bells attached. The ends of the collar were held together with Velcro.

"These are jingle bells, Buckley," she told me. "They're the same kind of bells that Santa's reindeer wear on their harnesses."

Let me tell you, that made my ears perk up! Did she say Santa had reindeer?

Gracie petted me on the top of my head. "But Santa's reindeer aren't regular reindeer. No, Santa's reindeer can fly. And they pull his sleigh through the sky on Christmas Eve. So he can bring presents to all the good kids and . . . well . . . cats, too."

Holy Catnip! Reindeer that could fly? And Santa's sleigh going through the sky? Suddenly my head started to spin, and I flopped over onto my side. I could hardly believe it. I'd learned so much about Christmas in one day that it was making me dizzy. Pretty soon my brain would be completely overloaded. Then I wouldn't be able to take in even one more thing.

Though I guess I shouldn't have been too surprised about the flying reindeer. After all, I had been told that Bogey could fly. So if he could fly, I suppose reindeer could probably fly, too.

Gracie moved from petting the top of my head and to scratching behind my ears. And boy, oh, boy, do I ever like to have the back of my ears scratched! It was exactly what a dizzy, overloaded cat like me needed. I closed my eyes and raised my head so she could get both sides. I was just starting to purr when she slid something around my neck. The next thing I knew, I heard the scratchy *scritch* sound of Velcro being fastened. And sure enough, she'd put one of the cat Christmas collars on me when I wasn't looking.

Gracie smiled at me. "See Buckley, now you've got jingle bells on, too. Just like Santa's reindeer."

Wow! Who would've ever guessed that I'd be just like Santa's reindeer? This was almost as good as when Bogey officially made me a cat detective.

My chest was bursting with pride, and I sat up straight and tall. Then I looked across the room and saw something that made my heart skip a beat.

It was the Princess. And she was staring at me with her big, green eyes.

Holy Mackerel! Talk about overloading my brain! Whenever she looked at me like that, it seemed like I couldn't remember anything.

"Oh, Buckley," she said. "You look so handsome in your red Christmas collar."

I sat up even straighter. Then I shook my head just to show off my collar even more.

"Jingle, jingle, jingle!" the bells on my collar rang out. The sound was so loud it made me jump. And when I say loud, well, I mean those bells were *really, really* loud!

Apparently they must have sounded pretty loud to the Princess, too. Because her eyes went wide and then she scampered off.

I turned to watch her go, and I heard "jingle, jingle, jingle" again. I turned the other way and I heard more jingling.

I jumped down off my chair and the jingling noise just kept on going and going. I ran across the room and the jingling didn't stop.

No matter where I went, or what I did, that jingling went on and on. And even when I sat perfectly still, I could hear that jingling in my mind.

How in the world did Santa's reindeer ever put up with this?

I ran into the dining room and saw Bogey waving at me from the entryway. I made a beeline for him.

He handed me a cat treat. "Take it easy, kid. Everything will be fine."

By then I could barely even see straight. I leaned downed to eat the cat treat and those jingle bells just kept on ringing.

I closed my eyes tight. "Oh, Bogey. How do I make this stop?"

I opened my eyes in time to see Bogey swipe down with a long, sharp claw. I heard the *rrrrrrippp* of Velcro being pulled apart. The collar fell to the floor with one last "jingle, jingle."

Then it was silent.

"Whew," I told Bogey. "Thanks for saving me. I would have gone crazy if I heard any more of that jingling."

Bogey grinned and handed me another cat treat. "Don't sweat it, kid. Rookie mistake. Stay away from Gracie when she's making her cat collars."

I nodded and munched on the treat. Now I wondered what we were going to do with that collar.

Before I could ask, Bogey glanced around the room and then looked at me. "What do you say we stash this collar back here for a while, kid? You never know when it might come in handy."

And before I could say a word, he had that collar out of sight. He slid it right behind the potted palm, in the same place where he hid an extra bag of cat treats.

I'm sure my eyes went pretty wide right about then.

Bogey moved away from the potted palm and rolled onto the floor. "Let's sneak any extra jingle bells out of Gracie's room, tonight, kid. So she can't put them on any more collars. She means well, and she sure loves us cats. But let's face it. No cat wants to live through all that ringing all Christmas long."

I had to say, that sounded like a pretty good idea to me. After all, I'd seen all the stuff she had on the kitchen table. And believe me, it looked like she had lots of other decorations she could put on those collars instead. Plus, I had to agree with Bogey — Gracie did mean well. She only wanted to make nice collars for cats. But she probably didn't know what it was like to have a whole bunch of bells ringing right next to her ears.

I was about to roll onto the floor and relax, myself, when I glanced into the darkness outside. That's when I saw the bright flashing lights in the distance.

Bogey saw them, too, because he suddenly stood at attention. "Hurry, kid! Follow me."

I didn't have time to ask him a single question. I just ran behind him, and we raced up the stairs to the spare bedroom on the second floor. We jumped up to a window where we had a perfect view of the entire street.

By now, sirens rang out in our neighborhood, and the lights came closer.

I gulped. "What is it?"

Bogey kept his keen eyes trained on the street. "Police cars, kid. Two of 'em. And they're headed right this way."

Holy Catnip!

CHAPTER 6

Holy Mackerel!

The sirens wailed even louder and those two police cars went rushing by!

Then they came to a screeching halt at the house just a few doors down from us. Bogey and I could barely see them from our spot in front of the window.

Downstairs, Gracie yelled, "Mom! Mom!"

And our Mom yelled back, "I'm here, honey!"

We heard the door to the garage open and slam shut.

"What's going on?" our Dad hollered.

After that came a bunch of garbled talking.

Finally we heard our Dad say, "It's the Nelsons' house. I'm going over to see if anyone is hurt. Or if they need help."

"Good idea," our Mom answered. "Gracie and I will come with you."

Bogey touched me on the tail. "C'mon, kid," he ordered. "We'd better get down there. And fast!"

I gulped. I wanted to ask more questions, but I didn't get a chance. Because Bogey turned and practically flew out of the room in a black streak.   I wasn't sure if I could even catch him.

But one thing was for sure — I had to try!   So I leaped from the windowsill and landed in the middle of the floor.   I raced after him and ran for all I was worth. It's a good thing I'm such a big cat, since I can cover a lot of ground in a short time.

I caught a glimpse of Bogey as he turned at the top of the stairs.   Seconds later I was on his tail as he zigzagged onto the staircase.   Then he took those stairs five at a time.   That's when I finally realized, Bogey really can fly!

I took the stairs a little bit slower and kept my eyes on my brother.

Finally, he leaped toward the potted palm in the front entry, just as our Dad and Mom and Gracie were walking out the front door.   As Gracie started to pull the door shut behind her, Bogey slid my jingle bell collar out from behind the potted palm.   He stuck the collar between the door and the doorjamb, only seconds before Gracie finished pulling the door shut.

But the door didn't close all the way.   The collar had stopped it from shutting completely.   And our human family had gone outside without noticing a thing.

I saw it all as I loped up to join Bogey at the door.

Holy Catnip!   I could hardly believe how smoothly he'd slid that collar into place.   Those bells didn't jingle one bit!   Clearly Bogey had some experience when it came to dealing with jingle bells.

I looked down at the collar that was wedged tightly in place.   A few of the jingle bells had been smooshed when Gracie closed the door on them.   Though to tell you the truth, I didn't think I would miss those broken jingle bells one bit.

Bogey grinned at me.   "Whew, kid.   That was a close one."

I'm sure my eyes were gigantic.   "It was?"

He nodded. "Yup, kid. I made it just in the nick of time. Otherwise, we wouldn't even have a prayer of getting this door open."

I stared at my brother. "Open the door? Why would we want to open that door?"

Bogey hooked a claw into the collar. "Because we need to go out and investigate, kid."

Suddenly I found it kind of hard to breathe. "But we're housecats. We're not supposed to go outside by ourselves. Gracie wouldn't like it if we went out. Our Mom wouldn't either."

Bogey looked to the top of the door and then back down again. "Well, kid, you know what they say. Desperate times call for desperate measures."

I scooted in closer. "They do?"

Now Bogey pulled gently on the collar. "Yup, kid. It's our job to protect our family. And we've gotta do whatever it takes to keep them safe. And solve this case."

I nodded at my brother. "Um, okay. But do we have to go outside to do that? Couldn't we just investigate from inside our house?"

Bogey shook his head. "No can do, kid. We need to find out what's going on out there. I've got a hunch there's been another break-in."

I leaned down to get a better look at what he was doing. "You do?"

He tugged a little harder on the collar. "You got it, kid. Now, can you give me a paw here and help me pull this open?"

"Uh, okay," I told him.

I reached out my right paw and hooked my claws under the door. While Bogey pulled on the collar, I used all my strength to pull the door open from the bottom.

Little by little, we got that door open wide enough for us to slip through. But first Bogey slid the collar back behind the potted palm. Then he darted out while I held back.

He stopped and turned to me. "What is it, kid?"

I blinked as the chilly air hit me in the face. "What if we get locked outside?"

Bogey grinned. "Don't sweat it, kid. We won't go far. We'll be back inside the house before you know it. Besides, we've gotta keep an eye on the door. To make sure no burglars run in while we're outside."

My heart suddenly felt like it was in my throat. "Burglars, out there?" I squeaked.

Bogey tiptoed over to the porch steps. "You never know, kid. So we've got to be extra careful. And we'd better get a move on before our humans get back."

Now my heart started to pound really loud and really fast. I knew Bogey was right. We had to hurry up and investigate, or it would be too late.

I poked my head out and glanced around. The neighbors from all over were gathering in the street. It was high time for me to go outside, too.

I put one paw on the front porch. The wood on the porch felt cold. But the wood on the floor inside our house felt nice and warm. Right at that moment, it seemed to me that nice and warm was a whole lot better than cold and breezy. I looked back at the hallway, where pretty lights blinked on our Christmas tree. I wanted to go sit under that tree, where I knew I'd be safe. I especially didn't want to go running around outside where burglars might get us!

Holy Mackerel!

I swallowed hard. A good cat detective was supposed to be brave. Really brave. But sometimes it's hard to be brave when you're really just a big scaredy-cat deep down inside. The only problem was, I wanted to protect my family and solve this case. And I didn't want to let Bogey down. That meant I had to *act* like I was brave, even though I wasn't.

So I shut my eyes and counted to three. When I hit number three, I jumped outside.

"Good going, kid!" Bogey meowed. "Now follow me. And keep low so nobody spots us."

The cold wind ruffled my fur as I scurried along behind my brother. It was dark out, which makes it a lot easier for black cats like us to stay hidden. Still, our porch light and the streetlights were on, so someone could have spotted us. That meant we had to be stealthy.

Bogey glanced around, and then we made a beeline for the big maple tree in our front yard near the street. Surrounding the tree were some big rocks and smaller shrubs, and we hid in the middle of it all. From there we had a perfect view of the hubbub going on a few doors down from us.

And what a bunch of hubbub it was! Holy Catnip! Neighbors were gathered in groups and chatting away. The red, blue, and white police car lights flashed in the darkness. They were so bright that I thought they would blind me whenever I looked at them.

Four police officers in uniforms were busy asking questions and looking around the house. Officer Smiley was talking to Mr. Nelson and taking notes in her notebook.

I pointed one of my big paws toward the house and accidentally swiped some leaves off a shrub. "Look! Isn't that Mrs. Mitchell? With her arm around Mrs. Nelson?"

Bogey squinted his eyes. "Sure is, kid. Sure is. The Mitchells live right next-door to the Nelsons. Looks like the Nelsons had a break-in, too."

Another break-in? And this one even closer to home? First the Mitchells' house and now the Nelsons'. The Nelsons lived only four doors down. As far as I was concerned, these break-ins were getting way too close to our house.

I shivered at the thought and snuggled down into the soft dirt.

Meanwhile, we watched our Mom and Gracie join Mrs. Mitchell and Mrs. Nelson. Our Mom gave Mrs. Nelson a hug.

Right about then, I sure wished someone would give me a hug. I wished I was safe and sound in Gracie's arms, where I could tuck my head in and close my eyes.

Instead, the cold wind blew into my huge ears and bent my whiskers back.

Beside me, Bogey didn't seem bothered by the breeze or the cold or the danger one bit. I only hoped I could be even half as brave as he was one day.

He nodded toward the scene. "Look at the front door, kid. Tell me what you see."

I did as he told me. But all I could see was a nice, red front door. It looked clean and bright, like a welcoming entry into the Nelsons' hundred-year-old house.

Then suddenly it hit me. "Didn't we see a Christmas wreath on that door? When we came home from the Mitchells'?"

Bogey gave me a paw bump. "Good job, kid! You've got it. I'm guessing the crook took the Christmas wreath, too."

I shook my head. "Wow. Who in the world would take a Christmas wreath?"

Bogey squinted his eyes. "A pretty rotten crook, that's for sure, kid. And a pretty smart one. Especially since I'm guessing they broke in from the back. I don't see any broken windows or doors from here."

I took another look, and sure enough, Bogey was right.

I tried to hunch down a little bit more. "Do you think it's the same crook who broke into the Mitchells' house?"

Bogey stood a little taller. "We can't tell for sure, kid. But I'd bet a bag of cat treats that it's the same criminal mastermind."

I shuddered. "I wonder what else they took."

Bogey frowned. "My money's on the Christmas presents, kid. Bet the burglars got them all. But we've got to find out for sure. We need to see the scene of this crime, too."

Suddenly my heart started to pound really loud again. Did Bogey actually expect us to run all the way over to the Nelsons' house? Right now?

I looked directly at my brother. "Um, uh, Bogey . . ."

Bogey chuckled. "Don't sweat it, kid. We're not going over there tonight. We've got to get back inside. Our humans could come home any minute now."

"Okay," I told him and turned to go.

"Stay low, kid," he meowed from behind me. "And be stealthy."

Well, I knew exactly how to be stealthy. And believe me, Bogey sure didn't have to tell me twice to get back inside the house. I zoomed back so fast I even beat Bogey there. I leaped up the porch stairs and slipped right through that narrowly open door.

Holy Catnip!

I don't think I'd ever been so happy to see my house again. I looked up at those twinkling Christmas tree lights and I felt warm all over.

Behind me, Bogey called out. "Hey, kid, over here. I could use a little help."

I turned to see him trying to push the front door closed. Unfortunately for Bogey, he was just too light to put much weight into it. But I, as a Maine Coon cat, had lots of weight to get that thing pushed shut.

In fact, I simply got a running start and leaped up on the door with my front paws. And sure enough, that door closed with a solid *thud*. For once in my life, my big, giant paws really did come in handy!

And not a moment too soon.

Seconds later, Gracie opened the door and walked in, followed by our Mom and Dad. They were all talking at the same time, and frowning. Gracie even looked like she was about to cry. She came right over to me and picked me up. Then she buried her head into my shoulder. I could feel her hot tears on my fur, so I wrapped my arms around her neck and gave her a good hug.

"Gee, Buckley, you feel kind of cold," she said as she sniffled into my fur.

I snuggled in tight and started to purr. Just to make her feel better.

It always made me sad when Gracie was sad.

Our Mom shook her head. "It's the same as the last burglary."

Our Dad locked the front door. "What an awful thing to go through at Christmastime."

Our Mom pulled the front curtains closed. "Who would do such a thing?"

Our Dad knelt down to pet Bogey. "I don't know, Abby. But until this crook is caught, we need to be extra careful. Let's make sure all the doors and windows are locked at all times."

"Sounds like a plan," our Mom nodded.

Then she turned to Gracie. "Time for bed. You've got school in the morning."

Gracie put me down and headed upstairs. Her face was streaked with tears and she kept her head down. Our Mom put her arm around her and walked her to her room.

I watched her go and suddenly my chest felt very, very heavy. Even kind of painful. If Gracie felt this bad when a neighbor's house was broken into, how would she feel if our house was broken into?

That's when I knew I had to work extra hard to protect my family. After all, they'd adopted me and given me this wonderful home and lots of love, too. Because they did that for me, I always like to do what I can to repay the favor.

Our Dad left us and headed into the kitchen. First he packed up Gracie's sewing stuff and took it up to her room. Then he came back downstairs and locked all the doors. Finally, he turned off the lights and headed for bed.

Once our whole family was upstairs, Bogey pulled his secret stash of cat treats out from behind the potted palm.

Pretty soon it would be time for us cats to run surveillance on the house to keep our family safe. Yet even though I'd run surveillance on our house a million times, tonight the idea of it made me nervous. Very nervous. And a little scared, even.

Especially since we knew there was a burglar out there on the loose.

I looked at my brother. "How will we ever catch this criminal mastermind?"

He handed me a treat. "The scene of the crime will tell us more, kid."

I munched on the treat. "The scene of the crime? How would we get to the scene of the crime?"

Bogey grinned at me. "Don't worry, kid. I've got a plan."

I blinked a couple of times. "You do?"

He nodded. "Yup, kid. Our Mom and Gracie will take us tomorrow evening. Right before dinner. Just like tonight."

I looked at him cross-eyed. "They will? But we don't even know if our Mom will be making casseroles again tomorrow. Especially since she's got to work at her store all day."

Bogey grabbed the cat treats and pranced into the home office. "Doesn't matter, kid. She won't need a casserole."

Sometimes I wondered if Bogey needed to lay off the cat treats. Because he sure wasn't making a whole lot of sense at the moment.

I followed him into the office. "She won't?"

Bogey jumped up on the desk and booted up the computer. He helped himself to another cat treat and passed one to me, too.

Then he turned to me and grinned. "I've got it all figured out, kid. By tomorrow night, we'll be taking a good look at that crime scene."

I jumped on the desk beside him. "We will?"

He handed me another treat. "Yup, kid. But first I've got to get it all set up."

I chewed on my cat treat and watched my brother. What in the world was Bogey planning? I was just about to ask him for the details, when my eyelids suddenly felt like they weighed about a million pounds. They dropped shut, and I flopped over on my side.

To tell you the truth, I wasn't sure if I could take a lot more excitement. Because, in one short day, I had learned tons about Christmas, investigated a crime scene, and sneaked out onto the front yard. That was an awful lot of stuff for one young cat in one day. Even if I was an oversized guy.

More than anything, right at that moment, I wanted to take a nice, long nap.

But I knew I couldn't. Because for me, the night was just beginning. Now I had to run surveillance and keep watch for burglars.

Holy Mackerel!

CHAPTER 7

"Wake up, kid. Wake up." I heard Bogey's voice and I felt someone shaking me. "Time to get to work."

I bolted upright.

Holy Mackerel! Had I fallen asleep? A good cat detective never falls asleep on the job!

"Detective Buckley Bergdorf reporting for duty," I announced to the room. I tried to salute but I only ended up poking myself in the eye.

"Take it easy, kid," Bogey said.

I looked around and glanced into the hallway. "Did I sleep for very long?"

Bogey stretched out his front legs. "Nope, kid. Maybe a half hour or so. Just enough time for me to put my plan into place."

I rounded out my back and stood on all fours. "Oh, good. I wanted to ask you about your plan."

Bogey trotted across the desk. "Sorry, kid. It'll have to wait. Right now we've gotta get a move on."

I blinked a few times and tried to wake up a little more. "We do?"

He jumped off the desk. "That's right, kid. We've gotta sneak those jingle bells out of Gracie's room. Then we've gotta run our first surveillance of the night. With burglars out there, we'll be running twice as much surveillance."

I jumped off the desk and followed him out of the office. "Oh, okay."

We ran through the hallway, raced up the stairs, and then headed straight for Gracie's room.

We were just a few inches from her door when Bogey stopped and held up his paw. "Okay, kid, time to be extra quiet. So we don't wake her up."

I nodded without saying a word.

Then I followed Bogey as we tiptoed into Gracie's room, single file. Luckily, Gracie was sound asleep and snoring softly.

Bogey glanced around the room. "Hmmm . . . I figured Lil Bits would be in here, kid," he whispered. "She usually spends her nights watching over Gracie."

Lil was another cat detective who was part of our family. She'd been adopted from the cat shelter years and years ago, and she'd been a cat detective even longer than Bogey! Lil had retired for a while, and she only recently started back on the job again. It was said she had once been one of the best cat detectives in the business. And even though she didn't work full-time, she helped us out when we needed her.

Bogey pointed to a pile of things on the window seat on the other side of the room. "Over there, kid. Looks like that's where our Dad put Gracie's sewing stuff."

So Bogey and I padded over and jumped up onto the window seat. Gracie had left her curtains open, and I took a quick peek outside. A few snowflakes filled the air. And though I wasn't sure, I thought I saw something move in the shadows of the streetlamp. It was at the neighbors' house, three doors down.

Right next to the Nelsons' house.

I gulped. "Bogey, did you see that?" I meowed as low as possible.

Bogey sprang to attention. "What is it, kid?"

I pointed out the window. "Outside. The house next to the Nelsons'."

Bogey pressed his nose against the glass. "What did you see, kid?"

I moved closer to the pane. "I don't know for sure. I thought I saw something move."

Together we sat there, just looking for a few minutes. But nothing else happened outside. I began to wonder if I'd seen anything at all. Maybe I was so nervous about burglars that I was starting to imagine things.

"I don't see it anymore," I told Bogey. "Maybe it was some leaves blowing around."

Bogey squinted and scanned the street once more. "Never doubt what you see, kid. Now let's get these jingle bells out of here. So we can get to our surveillance. I have a feeling it's going to be an interesting night."

Holy Mackerel! If I was nervous before, it was nothing compared to how I felt right now!

I watched while Bogey dug through Gracie's sewing stuff. Seconds later, he carefully pulled out a small plastic bag full of jingle bells.

I had to wonder, how were we going to get those bells out of there without making a huge racket?

But obviously Bogey already had that figured out. He pulled a square of fabric from the pile. Then he slid the bag of bells into the center of the fabric square.

"Bring all the corners up, kid," he instructed me.

I did just as he said.

"Now take all those corners into your mouth," he told me. "And stand up very, very slowly. Don't let those bells move much or they'll jingle."

It wasn't easy, but I managed to pick up all four corners. And before long, I realized I had formed kind of a little fabric bag for those jingle bells.

Then I inched up, very slowly and very carefully. Until I stood at my full height. All the while, I kept on holding that bag in my mouth.

Bogey jumped down from the window seat. "Good job, kid. Now comes the tricky part."

The tricky part? I thought this was the tricky part. Holy Catnip!

Bogey stood on his hind legs and put his front paws onto the edge of the window seat. "Okay, kid. Here's what I want you to do. Lean over but keep your weight on your back legs. Let your front paws come down to the floor. Then inch forward and balance on your front legs. After that, move your front legs forward until you can bring your back feet down. And try not to let those jingle bells bounce. Got it?"

I would have looked at my brother cross-eyed, but I knew I had to keep my head straight. I couldn't risk having those bells make a single sound.

So I did exactly what he told me. I moved to the edge of the window seat. Then I sat on my haunches, and little by little, I brought my front feet forward. Toward the floor.

And let me tell you, this was one time when it sure did pay to be an oversized cat. Because, before long, I had my front legs stretched out and my paws touched the ground. Then I walked forward with my front legs. I stopped when I had enough room to bring my back legs down.

I brought one leg down and was all ready to bring the other leg down. And that's when Gracie rolled over and yawned.

Oh, no! Had we woken her up?

Bogey signaled for me to hold still. So I froze in place. Like a big fuzzy cat statue with one leg hanging on the window seat and a cloth bag of jingle bells hanging from my mouth. I barely even breathed right about then. But my heart was pounding so loud I was afraid Gracie might hear it. I was also pretty scared that I wouldn't be able to hold that position much longer.

But luckily, a few seconds later, Gracie started to snore quietly again. I wanted to breathe a huge sigh of relief but I would have dropped the bag if I did. Instead I held my breath.

Now Bogey signaled for me to move completely off the window seat. So I brought my last leg slowly down to the floor.

"Okay, kid," Bogey said. "You've gotta move very smoothly across the room. Don't turn your head. Be careful not to rattle those jingle bells. Or they'll make enough noise to wake everyone from here to Timbuktu."

And oh, how I knew exactly what kind of noise those jingle bells could make!

I followed Bogey across the floor and through the door of the room. I moved in slow motion and walked very evenly so those bells didn't make a sound.

Once we were outside the room, Bogey said, "Okay, kid, I'll take it from here. You head downstairs and start your surveillance."

I put the bag of jingle bells down on the floor. And that's when it hit me. I remembered the receipt I'd put in Gracie's coat when we were at the Mitchells' house earlier in the day. Until now, I'd forgotten all about it!

"Just a minute," I told Bogey.

Then I quietly padded back into Gracie's room. I found her coat lying across a chair. I stuck my big paw into the pocket and pulled the receipt out. For once my big paw had gone in exactly the direction I wanted it to go!

I grabbed the receipt in my mouth and trotted out to Bogey.

"Here," I told him. "I found this at the Mitchells' house. I don't know if it means anything. But maybe it's a . . ."

"Clue," Bogey finished the sentence. "Nunzio's store," he muttered. "A receipt for Christmas cookie cutters. Hmmm . . ."

I pointed to the bottom of the receipt. "Read this."

Suddenly Bogey's eyes went wide. "If you don't bring me some cookies," he read, "I'll just have to steal some."

I nodded. "Do you think he meant it?"

Bogey put the receipt with the jingle bells. "Could be, kid. Could be. In any case, I think we'd better investigate. We'll get our Mom to take us to work with her one day. Then we'll pay Nunzio a little visit."

I'm sure my eyes went as wide as the round ornaments on our Christmas tree. "Really?"

Bogey grinned. "Oh yeah. Who knows? You might have cracked the case. You did good, kid."

"Wow," I breathed.

Bogey glanced down the hall. "You'd better get downstairs and start your surveillance. I'll take the upstairs. We'll meet in the office when we're done."

He grinned at me and saluted. Perfectly. His paw just touched the top of his brow for a second, and then he pulled his arm away.

"Aye, aye," I said in return.

I tried to salute him back, but I hit myself in the mouth instead. I guess I was back to having trouble getting my paws to go where I wanted them to go again.

"See you in the office, kid," Bogey said before he turned to go.

I ran straight for the stairs. Seconds later, I was standing all alone in the hallway near the front door. Funny, but the downstairs of the house seemed really, really quiet now. And it felt kind of big and lonely and dark, too.

Holy Catnip!

Suddenly my heart pounded even louder than before, and I felt nervous all over again. I started to shake just a little bit.

It wasn't the darkness that bothered me so much. After all, cats can pretty much see in the dark. No, what worried me most was something that Bogey had told me once. He said that burglars and bad people came out at night. That's because it was easier for them to hide from other humans in the dark.

Now as I walked past the front door, every hair on my back and tail stood on end. I looked around, listened for any noises, and then took a good sniff. But everything was just as it should have been.

Then I moved on to the windows and checked them out. Everything appeared to be fine there, too. I tiptoed into the dining room and sniffed around those windows as well. I pulled back one of the curtains and took a good look outside. Big, fluffy snowflakes fell to the ground and shimmered in the streetlights. For a minute I sort of got hypnotized just watching all those flakes floating in the air.

But then something caught my eye. A shadow in the distance. Moving slowly over the lawn of the house across the street.

Was it a burglar? Whatever it was, this was one of those things I needed to tell Bogey about. And right away.

I dropped the curtain back in place. I had started to turn around when I heard it. A creaking noise. From right behind me!

Let me tell you, I jumped so high I thought I was going to hit the ceiling! When I landed, I saw it was only Lil Bits standing there behind me.

Part of me felt a gigantic wave of relief. But another part of me was still shaking.

Lil saluted me with a white paw. "Good evening, Detective Buckley. I apologize if I may have startled you."

I tried to thunk my paw to my chest, hoping to stop my heart from pounding so loud. Instead I only poked myself in the chin.

Lil is a white cat with black spots, and to be honest, she looks more like a linebacker than a cat. Bogey once explained to me that Lil is a British Shorthair. Apparently they're cats with wide bodies and short legs. Watch out if they ever tackle you!

I flopped on the floor and breathed a really big sigh.

Lil started to laugh at me but then she stopped herself. Lil was like that. She always called me "Detective Buckley," and she always showed me a lot of respect. She seemed to understand that I was still pretty new to the job and that I was only doing my best. Even if I wasn't as good as Bogey or Lil at being a cat detective yet.

I'd have to remember to act just like she did someday when I was the older detective and I was teaching a rookie the ropes.

"Thanks, Lil," I said. "I guess I'm just on edge with all the break-ins."

Lil nodded her round head. "As well you should be, Detective Buckley. It's times like this when it pays to be on guard. How about if I hang out with you for a while? We can make a few surveillance runs together."

I smiled at Lil. "Wow, that would be great, Lil."

I especially liked the idea of not running surveillance by myself tonight. It was a lot easier for a guy to be brave when he had someone with him for the scary stuff.

I bounced up on my feet and together we checked out every door and window on the first floor.

I was finally starting to relax a little bit when we heard it. At first I thought I was just imagining things. But when I noticed Lil's ears had perked up, I knew she'd heard it, too.

It was kind of a bumping sound. Then a scratching noise.

Coming from the front door.

Something or someone was out there. And it sounded like they were trying to break in.

Had the burglars shown up at our house?
Holy Catnip!

CHAPTER 8

Holy Mackerel! Someone or something kept bumping up against the front door. And then they started scratching, too. Were the burglars out there and trying to break in? Lil made a beeline for the front door and I followed. I sure was glad she was there with me, since I wasn't completely sure what to do in a situation like this one. After all, I was barely more than a rookie when it came to being a cat detective.

The bumping and scratching noise kept going.

"Stand ready," Lil told me. "We'll attack them the minute they break in."

She hunched down, ready to spring up and jump on any intruders.

I did the same thing. Though it was kind of hard to stay in that position. Especially since I couldn't stop shaking.

Seconds later, I heard Bogey padding his way downstairs in a hurry. He didn't even ask us why we were crouched like that. He somehow seemed to know already.

"I'll take the top of the tree," he told us. "I'll jump on 'em from here."

"Sounds good," Lil said. "Everyone attack if the burglars set one foot inside this house. That means all claws on 'full extension.' Scratch all you can and don't be afraid to bite."

Right about then, I think my jaw practically dropped to the floor. Did she say bite? I'd never bitten anyone in my life. Holy Catnip! I only hoped I could do it.

Now the thumping noise got louder and louder.

Then we heard it. The sound that made my fur stand on end.

"Bogey! Buckley!" A voice cried out. "Are you home? Let me in!"

I rolled my eyes. "It's Hector."

Lil groaned and stood up straight. "Hector. What in the world is he doing here?"

Bogey sighed and started to climb down from the tree. "Better hide the Princess. I just saw her upstairs in the sunroom with Miss Mokie. She'll be fine as long as she stays there."

"I'm on it," Lil said. She turned and zoomed up the stairs. I was amazed that such a round, stocky cat could run so fast.

"Buckley? Bogey? Are you there?" Hector hollered from the other side of the front door. And when I say hollered, I do mean hollered.

Hector is the Siamese who lives across the street and down a few doors. And if there's one thing that Siamese cats are famous for, it's the way they holler. And talk. And talk and talk and talk. In fact, Hector is known around the neighborhood for being a blabbermouth. A big blabbermouth. That's because he absolutely loves to find out any juicy gossip about anyone else. And whenever Hector gets any juicy gossip on *anyone*, well, he quickly passes that on to *everyone*.

Unfortunately, we had something at our house that we didn't want him blabbing about. You might say we hadn't exactly been broadcasting that the Princess had come to live with us. After all, she was still kind of "in hiding" from her old abusive humans. We didn't want them to figure out where she was and come looking for her one day. When they got out of jail, that was.

So why was Hector on our front porch now? Especially at this time of night and in this cold weather?

"Hello, Hector," I said through the door. "What are you doing here?"

Hector bumped against the door again. "What's going on in there, Buckley? I can hear voices. What are you guys talking about? I want to know."

I shook my head and moaned. "It's none of your business, Hector."

"Are you keeping secrets from me, Buckley?" Hector hollered even louder. "If you are, you might as well spill it. I always find out everything."

Remember how I told you that Lil showed me a lot of respect? Well, Hector showed me the exact opposite. He didn't show me any respect at all.

And it was starting to make me a little mad.

"I haven't got anything to spill, Hector. And even if I did, I wouldn't spill it to you. Now, tell me why you're really here or I'm leaving. I've got things to do. Important things."

Hector snickered. "Can you let me in, Buckley? I can't get in my house and it's cold out here."

"Sorry," I told him. "But our house is all locked up. How come you're outside tonight anyway?"

"I sneaked out of my house earlier," Hector said. "When they had the big robbery at the Nelsons' house. I absolutely had to see what was going on. So I popped out through the doggy door. I crossed the street and I ran all around the Nelsons' yard. But when I got back home, my family had already locked the doggy door. And they'd already gone to bed."

Okay, when he told me all that, I had to say, I felt kind of sorry for the guy. After all, Bogey and I had been outside checking out the burglary, too. And if things hadn't gone our way, we could have been the ones locked out instead.

Even so, we couldn't let Hector into our house, or he'd find out about the Princess. And we couldn't just leave him outside, either, since it was so cold.

I looked to Bogey and shrugged. "What can we do?"

Bogey motioned toward the office. "Not a problem, kid. We'll send a call from our Mom's computer to Hector's house. I'll type in a message and play it back with our speech converter. It'll tell them to let Hector in."

My mouth fell open wide. "We can do that? Wow. I'll let Hector know."

Bogey held up his paw. "Not so fast, kid. First let's see what Hector knows about the break-in. The guy was right there in the yard. Maybe he learned something."

I nodded at my brother. "Oh, right. That sounds like a good idea. But how do we get him to tell us what he saw?"

Bogey grinned. "It won't be hard, kid. All we have to do is get him started. Then he'll blab everything he knows. You know how he likes to talk."

I wrinkled up my forehead. "I know. He always acts like he's so much better than me because he knows something that I don't."

Bogey nodded. "Don't sweat it, kid. Use it to your advantage. Just let him play right into your paws."

Now I grinned back. "Oh, okay. Sounds like a plan."

Outside, Hector hollered some more. "Are you guys going to help me out, or what? What kind of neighbors are you?"

"Bogey is just figuring it out," I meowed back to Hector. "Wow, that must have been something! Running around the Nelsons' yard! I wish Bogey and I could have been there."

"Ha-ha!" Hector taunted me. "You had to stay home. You sure missed a lot!"

"Really? Like what?" I asked in my most innocent voice.

"Oh, all kinds of stuff," Hector told us. "There was wrapping paper all over the yard on the side of the house. Of course, that's where the burglars broke in. On the side of the house."

"Really?" I encouraged him. "Which side? Our side, or the Mitchells' side?"

"The Mitchells' side, of course," Hector said with a sneer in his voice. "If you had been there, you would have known that. It looks like the burglars took some of the stuff they stole out the same window they broke in to. But it also looks like they took some other stuff out the back door, too."

"That's interesting. What else did you find out?" I asked him.

Now his voice got kind of singsong-y. "Ha-ha! I was there and you weren't! I heard the humans talking and they said that Mrs. Mitchell is the one who called the police. And I heard her tell the police that she saw the break-in from her window. So she called them. But she was really shook up and she could barely even speak."

"Wow," I said. "I'll bet she was upset."

I hated the idea of Gracie or my Mom being as upset as Mrs. Mitchell was. Just the thought of it made me even more determined to solve this case.

So I took a deep breath and tried to think of more questions to ask Hector to keep him talking. "What about Mr. Mitchell? And Mr. Nelson? Did they say anything?"

I could tell that Hector had puffed out his chest. "Mr. Nelson was really angry. He kept wondering who could have done something so mean. And Mr. Mitchell just stood to the side with his arms folded. He looked really tired."

"I'll bet Mr. and Mrs. Mitchell didn't sleep very well last night," I went on. "Especially after their house was broken into. So . . . is there anything else you can tell me?"

"Isn't that plenty?" he snarled. "I know a lot more than you guys do."

I winked at Bogey, who was working in our Mom's office just off the hallway. "You sure do, Hector."

Bogey grinned as he typed on the computer. "Sounds like he's told us all he knows, kid. Tell him to run on home while I get the call set up."

And I did just that. Seconds later, Hector was trotting across the street, without even telling us thank you. Bogey gave me a "paws up" to let me know the call had gone through. I ran to the dining room and pulled the curtains back, just in time to see the porch light at Hector's house go on. Then I saw the door open and Hector ran inside.

Bogey came up beside me and handed me a cat treat from his secret stash. He had a big grin on his face.

He glanced out the dining room window. "That worked out well, kid."

I felt my ears stand straight up. "It did?"

Bogey nodded and handed me another treat. "Yup, kid. Hector told us a lot."

I stared at Bogey with wide eyes. "He did?"

Bogey peered into the bag of treats that seemed to be running low. "Yup, kid. We found out there's probably more than one burglar. Two, at least. I'm betting one took stuff through the window and the other took stuff through the back door."

I swallowed the salmon-flavored treat and thought about it. "Oh, right," I said after I'd connected all the dots. "That makes sense."

Bogey reached way down into the bag and pulled out another treat. "Plus, kid, it looks like they stole the Christmas presents again."

"How can you tell?" I asked him.

"Easy, kid," he said. "There was wrapping paper all over the lawn. People wrap up their presents in special Christmas paper. And that paper must have torn off when the burglars took the presents through the window."

Holy Catnip! There were more Christmas presents stolen? Now the Nelsons were going to feel as bad as the Mitchells did. Whoever these burglars were, they had to be stopped! And soon!

Bogey licked the crumbs off his paws. "There's something I still can't figure out, kid. How did the burglars know the Nelsons and the Mitchells had already bought their Christmas presents? Lots of people haven't bought their presents yet."

"Hmmmm . . ." I murmured. I tried to put my paw to my forehead, to help me think better. But I only ended up bonking myself in my whiskers.

Still, I stared out the window and tried to come up with an answer to that question. Bogey must have been doing the same thing, since we both sat silently munching on our cat treats for a few moments.

And then it hit me! The receipt I found at the Mitchells' house!

Suddenly I was so excited I could hardly stand it. I started bouncing up and down. For once, I had figured out the answer before Bogey even did. Maybe I really was getting the hang of this whole cat detective business.

I waved my paw in the air. "I know! I know!"

Bogey grinned at me. "What is it, kid?"

"The answer! I think I know what it is! I think I know how the burglar knew both the Nelsons and the Mitchells had gone shopping for Christmas presents."

Right at that moment, I saw a strange look come over Bogey's face. He looked just like our Mom and Dad did when Gracie came home with A's on her report card. Bogey looked like he was . . . well . . . proud.

He thunked his paw to his chest, right above his heart. "Way to go, kid! I knew you'd make a great cat detective one day. Now tell me what you've got figured out."

For some reason, I couldn't stop dancing around the room. "Remember the receipt I found at the Mitchells' house? The one from Nunzio's Novelties and Knick-Knacks Shop?"

Bogey nodded. "Yup, kid. I remember."

I stopped dancing for just a few seconds. "What if the Mitchells shopped at Nunzio's store, too? What if they both bought their Christmas presents at his store?"

Bogey munched thoughtfully on a cat treat. "It could add up, kid," he finally said. "Nunzio could steal back the stuff that he sold to people. Then he could put that stuff back on his store shelves. It would just look like merchandise for sale. Nobody would know the difference."

"Uh-huh. Right," I agreed.

Though to tell you the truth, I really hadn't thought about the part where he put the stuff back on his store shelves. It was a good thing I still had an experienced cat detective like Bogey to work with.

Bogey stretched and glanced upstairs. "Well, one thing's for sure, kid. We've got to check out Nunzio's store. Just as soon as we can. But first we'll have to convince our Mom to take us to work with her. Then we'll sneak on over to Nunzio's."

I'm sure my eyes went pretty wide right about then. "Sounds like a plan," I managed to say.

Then I gulped. Was it possible we were about to go and pay a visit to a real, live crook? Someone who had burglarized our neighborhood? A true criminal mastermind?

I had been really scared tonight, when I thought that very criminal mastermind was trying to break into our house. So how would I feel if I purposely set paw into the same room as that burglar?

The thought of it made me start shaking all over again.

Holy Mackerel!

CHAPTER 9

Holy Mackerel! My head was still spinning as we ran surveillance one more time that night. I took the downstairs run and Bogey took the upstairs. Then, in the middle of the night, we switched. I ran the upstairs and Bogey took the downstairs.

Bogey said it would keep us more alert if we changed up our routine every once in a while. Though right at that moment, I wasn't exactly feeling very alert. We'd been up all night, and I was ready for a nap. In fact, I was looking forward to it. All that surveillance can really be tiring on a guy.

I was also looking forward to finding out about Bogey's plan to get us to the Nelsons' house. So we could take a look at that crime scene, too. In all our excitement during the night, I'd forgotten to ask him about it.

But it would have to wait until I had finished my upstairs surveillance run.

I trotted down the hallway to Gracie's room and took a peek inside. Lil was lying on Gracie's bed, keeping an eye on things. She waved at me and gave me a nod of her head.

I gave her a "paws up" and continued on my route. A half hour later, I had checked out all the upstairs rooms except for one.

The sunroom.

That's when I paused. Okay, stopped dead in my tracks is more like it. Funny, while I was really afraid of burglars, there were other things that kind of scared me, too.

And one of those "things" was in the sunroom, resting on a purple velvet couch.

Holy Catnip!

Actually, she wasn't a "thing" at all. Instead, she was a very, very, very old cat. So old you might even say she was ancient. And because she was so old, she'd been to lots of different places and seen lots of different things in her lifetime. Some said she'd even flown on an airplane once. Bogey told me she'd lived in five different states and two different countries.

But I guess that's what happens when you get to be old. It seems the more candles you count on your birthday cake, the more stuff you've learned in life. So by the time you get to be really, really, really old, you have all kinds of wisdom. And let me tell you, the old cat in the sunroom was known for her wisdom. That's why everyone just called her "The Wise One." Her real name was Miss Mokie.

Yet even though she'd become very wise, her joints were kind of stiff and achy. That meant she had a hard time getting around the house. So she mostly just stayed in the sunroom. That way she could feel the warmth of the sun as soon as it came up in the morning. The heat made her aching joints feel better.

For some reason, I always felt a little nervous when I was around Miss Mokie. Maybe it was because she was so smart that it seemed like she was almost reading my mind sometimes.

Or maybe it was because she was absolutely revered around our house. It was said she once ruled the roost with an iron paw.

I only hoped I would be as old and wise as she was one day.

I padded carefully to the sunroom door and paused to take a deep breath. Running surveillance on the upstairs of the house meant I had to go into the sunroom, too. That room had to be checked out just like every other room.

I closed my eyes and took another deep breath. Then I gathered up every bit of courage I could find, just to set paw in that room. It didn't help that I knew even Bogey felt a little nervous around The Wise One.

Still, I had a job to do. And I had to do it right. So I opened my eyes and stood up nice and straight. Then I stepped into the room.

Miss Mokie noticed me the second I walked in. She was a huge, gray cat with long fur. Her fur stuck out in a ruff around her neck that kind of made her look like a lion. And even though she was a little shaky these days, her green eyes were still bright and full of life.

As always, she was lounging on her couch. She raised a paw just as I stepped inside the room, letting me know that I should halt.

"Please identity yourself," she commanded me.

I bowed, just like Bogey had taught me to do. "It's me, Miss Mokie. Detective Buckley Bergdorf."

She nodded to me, like a queen nodding to her subject. "Ah, yes, young Detective. Please enter and partake of a drink." She pointed a paw in the direction of her private water dish.

I leaned over the dish and took a sip. It would have been rude not to. And us cats always used our very best manners around Miss Mokie.

When I stood up again, Miss Mokie motioned to the Princess, who was sitting across from her on another chair. "The good Princess Alexandra has kindly been keeping me company this fine winter night. It's been such a delight to have her join our family this year."

The Princess looked at me with her big, green eyes, and my heart made this funny *pat-a-pat-pat* sound. Suddenly, I forgot why I'd even come into the room.

"Hello again, Buckley," she said. "Do you like our pretty Christmas tree that went up today?"

All I could manage to do was nod and mumble, "Um-hum. I like it a lot."

Miss Mokie sat up, towering over us on her purple throne. "Are you here as part of your cat detective duties?"

I glanced around the room. "Yes I am, Miss Mokie. It's my turn to run surveillance on the upstairs of the house."

"Excellent," she said. "Simply excellent. But I sense something is troubling you, young Detective."

It was? I guess I hadn't really been aware of anything that was troubling me. Well, except for the break-ins and all the new stuff I'd learned in one short day. And then there was all the usual stuff that bothered me. Sometimes I worried about Gracie and sometimes I worried that Bogey would get into trouble.

But aside from that, the only thing that had really been bothering me was . . .

"I don't understand all this stuff about Christmas," I blurted out. The second I'd said it, I couldn't believe that I'd said it. For some reason, it just came bursting out of me.

Holy Catnip! What had I done?

The Wise One furrowed her brow. "I see. What is it that you don't understand?"

Before I could even think about it, more words rushed out of me like a big, giant flood. A flood I couldn't seem to stop.

"Well," I said. "I just found out about Christmas today. And I don't understand why it's so important to everyone. People are decorating or making cookies or

buying presents and all kinds of things. And Christmas
is so important that some people want to hurt other
people by stealing their presents. Because it seems like
stealing Christmas presents is worse than stealing any
other kinds of presents. So, why is Christmas so
important to everyone?"

The Wise One nodded. "Ah, yes, Grasshopper. I can
see where it would all be rather perplexing. And yes,
you are correct, Christmas is a very important day. And
the Christmas season is one of great celebration."

"But why?" I stood up straight and looked her in
the eyes. I couldn't believe how I was acting around one
so revered as the Wise One! Yet for some strange
reason, I couldn't seem to control myself.

And I couldn't seem to keep my mouth shut. "What
are we celebrating?" I went on. "Bogey says it's a
birthday party. Is it? And whose birthday is it?"

Miss Mokie gave me a small smile. Then she held
up her paw, as though asking for silence.

I hunched down, with my front legs before me.
Ready to listen to whatever wise words she might send
my way.

Miss Mokie looked from me to the Princess, and
then back to me again. "Ah, yes," she said. "You might
think of it as a birthday party. After all, Christmas is
the time when we celebrate the birth of baby Jesus. A
long, long time ago, Jesus was born in a stable in
Bethlehem. His Mother and Father had traveled for
many miles and many days to get to Bethlehem. And
when they arrived and tried to find a place to stay, there
weren't any rooms left in the whole city. So an
innkeeper let them stay in his stable, and that's where
Jesus was born. His Mom laid him in a manger filled
with straw, which made a nice soft bed for him."

I'm sure my eyes went really wide right about then.
"In a stable? With animals?"

Miss Mokie nodded. "Yes, that is correct, young
one. With animals."

I scooted a little closer to her. "Cats, too?"

The Wise One sat back on her haunches. "Ah, yes, amongst us cats there is a legend of a tabby cat who lived in the stable. And much like many cats desire to be helpful, this cat wanted to help care for the newborn baby Jesus. So the cat bathed and bathed and bathed himself first, so his fur was nice and clean and shiny. Then he climbed into the manger and cuddled in next to baby Jesus, to keep the baby warm. The cat started to purr nice and loud, and that made baby Jesus fall fast asleep. His mother, Mary, was very grateful to that tabby cat."

My mouth fell open wide. For once, no more words came out.

But Miss Mokie still had lots more to say. "On the night when Jesus was born, there was an enormous, bright star in the sky. The brightest and biggest star that anyone had ever seen. That star hung in the sky, right over the spot where Jesus was born. It lit up the night and burned brightly for many days. And it directed all to come see the baby."

"Wow," I breathed.

I noticed the Princess looked pretty wide-eyed, too. I could tell she was enjoying the story, just like I was.

"Did lots of people come to see the new baby?" the Princess asked.

Miss Mokie turned to her. "Oh, yes, they most certainly did. And they brought wonderful presents for the new baby. That's why we give presents to each other every year when we celebrate Jesus' birthday."

"Wow," I said again, just under my breath. "Bogey told me there'd be presents. I always like getting presents."

Miss Mokie turned back to me. "Just remember one thing, young Detective. It is more important to give presents than to receive them. It is only in giving that you can feel the true joy and spirit of Christmas."

The Princess and I looked at each other. I knew I wouldn't mind giving her a present. And I wouldn't mind giving one to Bogey, too. And to the rest of my family.

Before I could say another word, Miss Mokie raised her paw again. "You have learned much here tonight, Grasshopper. But now you must leave me. For it is time for me to rest."

I sat up straight. "Aye, aye, Miss Mokie. Thanks so much for answering my question." I tried to salute her but I ended up poking myself in the nose instead.

Miss Mokie closed her eyes and the Princess waved to me. I knew she would be staying with Miss Mokie while she slept. She seemed to like taking care of the most senior member of our household.

I finished my surveillance of the room on tiptoes, so I wouldn't make any noise. As I was leaving, I glanced back at the Princess once more. She smiled at me and I smiled back. There was something about hearing Miss Mokie tell the story of Christmas that made us both happy.

Then I ran out of the room and down the hallway. I felt like I was floating on air. I skipped down the stairs and went into our Mom's office, where I joined Bogey.

But now I started to think about something else the Wise One had said to me. That it was more important to give presents than to receive them. But what kind of presents could I give to the cats and the humans in my family?

"Everything okay up there, kid?" Bogey asked me. He'd been busy typing on the computer keyboard when I walked in.

"Uh-huh," I told him. "Everything is locked up and secure. No burglars to report."

He stopped what he was doing and handed me a cat treat. "Looks like we squeaked by tonight, kid. The humans will be getting up soon. And I don't think our burglars will be breaking in with so many people up and around."

I munched nervously on the treat. "That's good."

Bogey went back to his typing. "Did you have a little chitchat with Miss Mokie?"

I swallowed the treat. "Um-hum. Bogey, why does she always call us 'Grasshopper'?"

Bogey shook his head. "I don't know, kid. It's just something she does."

I scrunched down on the desk. "She told me to give presents for Christmas. But I don't know anything about giving presents."

Bogey grinned. "Don't sweat it, kid. You just give something you think the other cat or person would like."

I gulped. "But how would I know?"

Bogey stopped typing for a minute and waved a paw in the air. "It's easy, kid. Just think of something you would like. Lots of times, it's what the other person likes, too."

He grabbed another cat treat and handed one to me. Well, at least I knew one thing for sure — Bogey liked cat treats! That meant I could give him cat treats for Christmas. But trying to figure out to give everyone else, well, that was a different story.

So I thought of Bogey's advice about giving something I might like, too. And I sure liked cat toys. When I had time off, I spent hours chasing little furry toy mice, or fuzzy balls, or fake feathered birds. According to Bogey, if I liked it, others were bound to like it, too. Maybe cat toys would make good Christmas presents.

Bogey hit the "Print" button on the computer. A few seconds later a sheet of paper came jerking out of the printer.

I munched on the treat and pointed to the paper. "What's that?"

He grinned back at me. "Part of our plan to get to the Nelsons' before dinner tonight."

I gasped. I had been dying to ask Bogey about our plan. And I was just about to say something when I started to choke on my cat treat.

Bogey patted me on the back. "Take it easy, kid. Some of those cat treats can be a little stiff."

Then he pushed the paper from the printer and onto the floor. "Why don't you head into the kitchen for some water, kid? I've got to get this letter stashed away before our humans get out of bed."

He picked up the letter in his teeth and pranced out of the room.

I thunked my chest so I would quit choking. Did Bogey say "letter"? What was this letter? It looked like he'd just finished typing it himself. But why in the world did he have to stash it away? And how was it going to get us to the Nelsons' house tonight?

So many questions swirled around and around in my mind. It all made me a little bit dizzy. I wondered if I was up to the task of solving this crime. Maybe I didn't have what it took to get the job done.

But then again, it had been a really big day. And night. In fact, it seemed like two days in one. Or even three. Maybe it was kind of normal to feel like I was up to my whiskers in clues and questions and crime-solving right now.

I could hardly believe that we'd barely even started to investigate this case. And already things were getting complicated.

Holy Mackerel!

CHAPTER 10

Holy Catnip! The day began with lots and lots of hustling and bustling. Our Dad got up early and started getting ready for work. Then Gracie got up and started getting ready for school. And our Mom cooked breakfast while everyone else got ready. Since her store didn't open until ten o'clock, she usually went out the door a little bit later than everyone else.

She lined up plates of canned cat food for Bogey, Lil, the Princess, and me in the kitchen. We all dug in while she took a plate up to Miss Mokie. Since I was on the end of the row, I hunched down and tried to stay out of the way. Not an easy thing to do for an oversized cat like me. Still, I did my best. Because I had learned a very important lesson right away when I got adopted into this house — watch out for the humans on Monday morning!

That's because the humans all stumbled along, bleary-eyed and half awake, on that day and at that time. Sometimes they didn't see a tail on the ground or a cat sitting in their path. No, on Monday mornings, it was our job to watch out for them.

Even so, Gracie picked each of us up and kissed us good-bye before she headed for the school bus.

She gave me an extra special hug. "Today is a big day for me," she said. "Today we find out about the school Christmas play. And I'm trying out for the part of the angel."

I gave her a kiss on the nose. I couldn't think of a better person to play an angel than Gracie.

She giggled. "You've been a very good boy this year, Buckley. I'll bet Santa will bring you lots of presents."

There was that name again. Santa. The more I heard about him, the more I was dying to meet him.

Gracie put me down and buttoned up her coat. Then she opened the front door and she was off.

I had a feeling Santa was going to bring Gracie lots of presents, too. Because she had been really good herself. In fact, Gracie was always a good person.

Once she had closed the door, I flopped over on my side and closed my eyes. I was one tired guy after all the excitement of yesterday. And from running surveillance all night.

Bogey came up behind me. I opened one eye to see he had a big frown on his face.

"Looks like we won't be going to our Mom's store today," he told me. "I checked her schedule. It turns out she's got meetings around town first thing this morning. She'll never take us with her to a meeting."

I tried to open my other eye, but for some reason, it weighed so much that I couldn't even pull it open. "What are we going to do?"

"We won't sweat it, kid," he said. "We'll try again tomorrow. But we'll still see what we can find out at the Nelsons' tonight."

And that's when I remembered to ask him about his plan. There was only one problem. My other eyelid suddenly weighed a ton, too. I barely had time to drag myself from the front entry to a nice, sunny spot in the dining room — only seconds before that eyelid fell shut.

The next thing I knew, Bogey was shaking me on the shoulder. "Wake up, kid! Wake up!"

"Huh, what?" I grumbled. I opened my eyes to see my nice sunny spot had disappeared and it was now dark outside. Had I really slept through the whole day?

Bogey waved a cat treat over my nose. "Here, kid. This'll get you going. It's time to put our plan into place."

I took the treat from him. "What plan?"

Bogey shook his head. "C'mon, kid. Snap out of it. We're about to head over to the Nelsons' house. To check out the scene of the crime."

Oh, that plan!

Bogey started pacing across the hardwood floor. "I've already ordered the pizzas, kid."

Now I sat up and stretched. "Pizzas? How did you do that?"

He grinned. "Over the Internet, kid. With our Mom's computer. I paid for it with my emergency fund account."

Sometimes I forgot that Bogey had his own bank account. Before he became a cat detective, he'd made a bundle of money acting in cat food commercials.

I was about to ask him why he had ordered those pizzas, when I heard a commotion outside. The next thing I knew, Gracie and our Mom came through the front door.

Gracie squealed and made a beeline for me. She picked me up and immediately started spinning around the room. We went around and around and around.

As always, I just hung on for dear life.

"Oh, Buckley," she cried. "I got it! I got the part! I'm going to be the angel in the school play."

Right about then, I really wanted to give Gracie a kiss on the nose. But I was too busy watching the room fly by.

I could hardly wait for Gracie to grow out of her spinning phase.

She put me down and I wobbled to the front entry. Even though I'd stopped spinning, my eyes still kept on going in circles. I could barely make out Bogey pulling something from his secret stash behind the potted palm. Pretty soon I recognized that "something" as the letter he had printed out the night before.

He dropped it at our Mom's feet while she took off her coat.

Our Mom reached down to pet Bogey. "What have you got there, my handsome boy?"

She picked him up with one hand and the letter with the other.

Then she started to read aloud. "*Dear Abigail. That is so thoughtful of you to offer to bring us a pizza for dinner tonight. We heard you brought the Mitchells a casserole after their house got broken into. So bringing us a pizza after our house got broken into is really nice, too. What a kind, sweet, beautiful and wonderful person you are. And like I said, nice. Very nice. Your family is wonderful, too. Especially your two boy cats, Buckley and Bogey. They are really, really wonderful. Be sure to bring them with you when you bring the pizza. Signed, Mrs. Nelson.*"

As our Mom finished reading the letter, her mouth fell open wide. "I don't remember telling Nellie Nelson that I would bring over a pizza. Do you remember me telling them that?" she asked Gracie.

Gracie shrugged her shoulders. "I don't remember you saying anything like that. But it sure would be nice. And she already said how nice you were in her letter."

"Well, yes, it would be nice," our Mom agreed. "I guess I'll have to order a pizza then."

Our Mom held Bogey close to her face. "Bogey, where did you get this letter?"

But Bogey didn't so much as meow to her. Instead, he just started to purr.

"If I didn't know better . . ." our Mom said.

But she didn't even get a chance to finish her sentence. Because, just then, the doorbell rang.

"Pizza delivery!" A young man yelled from behind the door.

Our Mom's eyes went wide. "Pizza delivery? I don't remember ordering any pizzas . . ."

Gracie giggled. "Mom, maybe you've been working a little too hard."

Our Mom opened the door and accepted the pizzas. She signed for them quickly and gave the ticket back to the deliveryman.

Seconds after she did, she crinkled up her eyebrows. "Wait a minute . . . Did that ticket have the name 'Bogart' on it?"

But the pizza delivery guy just smiled and waved to her. "Don't worry, ma'am, the pizzas were already paid for." Then he jumped into his car and he was off.

Our Mom stood in the door for a second with her mouth hanging open.

Then Gracie tugged at her sleeve. "Mom, Mom. We'd better get a pizza over to the Nelsons before it gets cold."

Our Mom just kind of gasped and made a funny sputtering noise. She took one pizza and stuck it in the oven to keep it warm. Minutes later, we were all on our way to the Nelsons' house. Our Mom carried Bogey and the pizza, and Gracie carried me.

So this had been Bogey's big plan. And what a good plan it was! Holy Mackerel!

Bogey leaned over our Mom's shoulder and grinned at me. I grinned back and gave him a "paws up."

Then, before I knew it, we were inside the Nelsons' house. Mrs. Nelson was so thankful to see us. She kept gushing over my Mom and Gracie, telling them how thoughtful they were. She took the pizza from our Mom and set it on the coffee table in the living room.

Our Mom just sat on their couch with a confused look on her face. Gracie carried me over to see their Christmas tree in the corner.

Mrs. Nelson sniffed and blew her nose into a tissue. "I'm so glad we have such wonderful neighbors like you, Abigail. Would you mind if I held Bogey? What a beautiful cat he is. And he's smart, too."

She took Bogey into her arms.

Our Mom raised one eyebrow. "Oh, yes, he's smart all right, Nellie. Sometimes I wonder exactly how smart he is."

Bogey gave Mrs. Nelson a kiss on her nose. She smiled and tears started running down her face. She hugged him tight and he just purred and purred.

I guessed Mrs. Nelson was feeling really bad, too, after having her house broken into. And Bogey knew just how to make her feel better.

She smiled at my brother. "Oh, Bogey, you are such a joy. I could use a cat like you in my life."

Then she turned to our Mom. "I still can't believe someone robbed us. And right before Christmas, too."

Our Mom nodded in sympathy. "I can't either, Nellie. Did they steal a lot of stuff?"

"All our Christmas presents," Mrs. Nelson said. "And they took our front-door wreath and the crystal star from the top of our tree. Plus they took a bunch of our star ornaments and the big star I hang in my entryway every year. That star belonged to my grandmother. It can never be replaced."

Fresh tears rolled down her cheeks. So Bogey wrapped his arms around her neck and pushed his head beneath her chin.

He was still hugging her when Mr. Nelson came in from the kitchen. Mr. and Mrs. Mitchell followed him in.

All at once, everyone started saying hello to each other. Then Mrs. Mitchell walked over and sat by the Christmas tree. Mr. Mitchell joined her. He was a big guy with brown hair and hazel eyes. And to tell you the truth, he kind of blended into the background.

Mrs. Nelson, on the other hand, was the kind of lady who stood out in a crowd. She had black hair and dancing blue eyes. And she seemed to have a lot of energy.

She pointed to a plate of cookies on an end table. "Mike and Mesmeralda were so kind to bring us Christmas cookies."

I looked over and saw cookies in the shape of snowflakes, angels, Christmas trees and Christmas ornaments. There were bells and Santa Clauses and holly leaves and candy canes. Just like the cookies I'd seen at the Mitchells' house. Every one of them was decorated with icing in red, green, white, or blue. Let me tell you, each one of those cookies was a work of art. They were so pretty, someone could have hung them on the Christmas tree and they would have looked just like ornaments.

Our Mom smiled at the Mitchells. "That was so sweet of you. I'm sure it will help keep the Christmas spirit alive."

The Mitchells both frowned and didn't say a word.

Mr. Nelson ran his fingers through his gray hair and turned to our Mom. "I don't know what we're going to do. Our son and his wife and our grandkids are flying in right before Christmas. And all their presents are gone. We can't afford to buy more."

Our Mom tilted her head and gave Mr. Nelson the same look she gave Gracie when she'd scraped her knee. "Don't worry, Nate. The people of St. Gertrude are really good people. We'll all pitch in together and help you out."

Mrs. Mitchell sighed. "We don't have any Christmas presents under our tree either."

Mr. Mitchell put his arm around her. "Don't cry, Mesmeralda. At least we have our health."

Mrs. Nelson went over and put her arm around Mrs. Mitchell, too. "Christmas isn't just about presents, Mesmeralda. It's about so much more."

I smiled inside. I knew Mrs. Nelson was right. The Wise One had told me so last night.

"Don't worry, Mesmeralda," our Mom said. "The good people of St. Gertrude won't forget about you either. I sure hope these awful burglars are caught soon."

And speaking of catching burglars . . . I watched Bogey jump down from Mrs. Nelson's arms. He ran behind the Christmas tree without anyone noticing. But I knew exactly what he was doing. He was checking out the scene of the crime!

Holy Catnip!

I was about to jump down, too, when Gracie suddenly hugged me tighter and bounced to the center of the room. "Don't forget to come to the Christmas play at my school, everyone. That will help you get into the Christmas spirit! I'm going to be the angel."

Mrs. Nelson came over and gave Gracie and me a hug. "Good for you, dear. You'll be a wonderful angel."

Then she stood back and patted me on the head. "You're an angel, too, Buckley. Wish I had a cat like you, too."

That's when I climbed up Gracie's shoulder. I reached over to Mrs. Nelson and gave her a kiss on the nose.

Everyone laughed. Except for the Mitchells.

"Do you always take your cats everywhere you go?" Mrs. Mitchell asked quietly.

Our Mom stood up. "Not everywhere. But lots of places. And right now it's time for us to take them home. So Nate and Nellie can eat their pizza while it's still warm."

Mrs. Nelson smiled. "Well, I, for one, am happy you brought them over today. We always enjoy a visit from the boys."

Our Mom called to Bogey and he came running from behind the Christmas tree. She picked him up, and Mr. and Mrs. Nelson walked us to the door. They thanked us all again for the pizza.

A few minutes later, we were headed home. The streetlamps overhead lit the way.

"What did you learn?" I meowed to my brother.

He leaned up on our Mom's shoulder. "It was the same as yesterday, kid. I could smell everyone who was there, and maybe the slight scent of Officer Smiley. But no one else. These burglars are brilliant, kid. They've figured out a way to break in, steal stuff, and not leave a trace behind. Like I said, they're real criminal masterminds."

There was that word again. Criminal mastermind.

The idea of it made me shiver. I snuggled in tighter to Gracie. That was, until something caught my eye.

I popped my head up and stared at our own house, up ahead. Something was happening. There was a bunch of stuff on our front yard. And I could barely make out someone going in the front door.

Was it the burglars? Had they shown up at our house, too? Were we being robbed?

Holy Catnip!

CHAPTER 11

Holy Mackerel! My heart started pounding a million miles an hour. I hollered to my brother as he was being carried by our Mom.

"Bogey, Bogey!" I meowed as loud as I could. I tried to jump from Gracie's arms. I had to warn her and our Mom.

But Gracie just giggled. "Buckley, I'm not letting you down out here. I don't want you to get lost outside."

Bogey tilted his ears toward me. "What is it, kid?"

By now I was in such a frenzy that I could hardly get the words out. "Bogey . . . look! Our front lawn!"

Bogey closed his eyes and yawned. "Yup, kid. That's our front lawn up there, all right."

"But Bogey," I gasped. "I think the burglars are there. They're breaking in!"

Bogey glanced over at our house and then back to me. "Don't sweat it, kid."

Holy Catnip! Burglars were breaking into our house, and all Bogey could say was "don't sweat it"? I could hardly believe my ears. Right then and there, I was sure he'd been hitting the cat treats a little too hard. Or maybe he didn't get enough catnaps today and he wasn't thinking straight.

I tried to jump around in Gracie's arms, but she was holding on to me tight. No matter how much I tried to wriggle away, she wasn't going to let me go.

"Shouldn't we stop them?" I hollered. "Shouldn't someone call the police? Shouldn't we protect our Mom and Gracie?"

Bogey shook his head. "Nope, kid. It's not burglars. Nobody's breaking in."

"They're not?" I squeaked.

"Look again, kid," Bogey told me. "Our Dad just walked out the front door."

I took another look, and sure enough, the person who walked out was our Dad.

Bogey waved a paw my way. "He's just setting out the lawn ornaments, kid."

Right about then, I started to feel pretty dizzy. Lawn ornaments? I vaguely remembered Bogey telling me about lawn ornaments.

And now as we moved closer, I could see some big things cut out of wood sitting on the yard. Those things were painted and looked a lot like . . . people. People wearing robes.

I calmed down in Gracie's arms. "What is that?"

Bogey nodded to our front yard. "It's called a Nativity scene, kid. There's Joseph and Mary. They're Jesus' Mom and Dad. Then there's baby Jesus lying in a manger on a bed of straw. And there's some sheep and some other people, too."

I nodded back. "Oh, okay, I can see it now. What is that big wooden thing around it?"

Bogey grinned. "It's the outline of the stable, kid. It's supposed to show the night when Jesus was born. Pretty soon Dad will put up a big star that lights up. And he'll hang strings of lights from it that look like star trails. Plus he'll put up lots of other lights."

"Wow," I breathed.

Baby Jesus lying in a manger. I'd heard the whole story the night before from the Wise One.

Wow, this Jesus must be some guy.

A few minutes later, Gracie passed me to our Dad. "I don't know what's bothering Buckley. He sure is squirmy tonight."

Our Dad had his winter jacket on. The fleece felt nice and soft against my fur.

"Too much Christmas excitement for you, Buckley?" he asked as he held me in his arms.

Boy, he could sure say that again.

That night, our Mom and Dad and Gracie ate pizza while us cats ate our favorite food — tuna fish. Our humans talked mostly about the break-ins in the neighborhood. But then their conversation quickly turned to the Craft Fair on Saturday. Gracie wanted to make sure she had enough collars in enough different colors for people to buy. And our Dad talked about the last of the Christmas lawn ornaments he needed to paint. All in all, it sounded like they would be taking lots of stuff to the Craft Fair.

Once Bogey and I had finished our tuna, we lounged next to Gracie at the dinner table.

She reached down to pet me. "You and Bogey can come to the Craft Fair, too. You can model some cat collars and help me sell them."

Our Dad laughed. "I even have a little red wooden wagon for you that I made. It looks like a small version of Santa's sleigh, except it has wheels hidden below. Buckley can pull it and Bogey can ride in it. That way they'll help sell collars *and* lawn ornaments."

I turned to my brother, who had a huge grin on his face. "Watch out, kid. Soon they'll have us doing all kinds of things they think are cute."

I backed under the kitchen table. After all, I'd been down that road of having to be "cute" before. And believe me, there was nothing cute about it!

Later, after dinner, Gracie went back to sewing cat Christmas collars and our Mom and Dad finished decorating the front lawn. When they were done, Bogey and I just sat in the dining room and stared out the windows. I couldn't stop looking at all the pretty blinking lights. And I couldn't stop looking at what Bogey had called a Nativity scene.

But once in a while I looked back at the pretty Christmas tree in the hallway. It had blinking lights, too. Seems like we were surrounded by lots of pretty things.

Holy Mackerel. When Bogey said Christmas was the best, well, he wasn't kidding.

Bogey passed me a cat treat. "Here's a little dessert for you, kid. Hope you're ready for a lot of surveillance runs tonight."

"Aye, aye," I told him. But this time I didn't even try to salute him. I was just too busy looking at all the lights.

Later, after our humans had gone to bed, we did run surveillance. Lil even offered to help us and she ran a few shifts, too.

All in all, the night was pretty quiet. There wasn't a burglar in sight. And believe me, nothing could have made me happier.

In the morning, after Gracie had gone to school and our Dad had gone to work, Bogey insisted we head straight for the kitchen.

"No matter what, kid. We've gotta go to work with our Mom today," he told me.

I followed along behind him. "So we can investigate Nunzio's shop, right?"

Bogey made a beeline for the kitchen cabinets. "You got it, kid."

He jumped up on the counter and planted himself right across our Mom's purse! "Come on up and join me, kid. Today she's not going anywhere without us."

I ran up to the cabinet but I stayed on the floor.
"Um, I think I'll wait down here."

After all, I was a little nervous about jumping up on
the kitchen counter.   Especially since we weren't
actually supposed to go on the counter.   And I really
didn't want to get in trouble and end up in time-out.

Bogey grinned down at me.   "Suit yourself, kid."

He slipped a bag of cat treats into the pocket of her
purse.   "Like I said before, kid, desperate times call for
desperate measures.   Just look as adorable as you
possibly can.   Our Mom can never resist us when we
look adorable."

And sure enough, Bogey was right.   When our Mom
was ready to go, she ran into the kitchen to grab her
purse and her keys.   That's when she saw us.   At first
she kind of gasped.   Then she looked a little bit mad,
and finally she sighed.

"Let me guess," she said with a smile.   "You boys
want to come to the store with me today."

Bogey reached up and gave her a kiss on the nose.
And I rubbed up against her legs.

She laughed.   "I'll take that as a 'yes.'"

And minutes later, we were off.

It only took about fifteen minutes to get to our
Mom's store.   Her antique shop, Abigail's Antiques, was
probably the most popular antique store in downtown
St. Gertrude.

Our Mom carried us both in through the back door
and set us on the floor.   Because she took us to work a
lot, she already had an area in the back all set up for us.
We had our own food and water dish.   Plus a cat box,
beds, and toys.

Not that we had time to play with toys at her shop.
That's because the place was loaded with lots of old
furniture that was stacked all over the place.   And there
were rows and rows of shelves and display cases.   It was
a perfect place for cats like us to explore.

Nunzio's Novelties and Knick-Knacks Shop was located right next door. Our Mom had taken us over there once before. And we'd even wandered over a time or two on our own, without her knowing we'd been there. But generally speaking, we stayed away from the place. That's because Nunzio had made it clear he didn't like us. He was a big man with dark, dark eyes, and even darker hair. And believe me, when that man stared at me, well, it felt like his eyes were boring right into me. Kind of like he had laser beams instead of eyes.

But today, we didn't care whether he liked us or not. Today we were going over to investigate. The only problem was, first we had to sneak out of our Mom's store. Without her seeing us.

While our Mom went to the front of the shop, Bogey and I stayed in the back. The ladies who worked for her, Millicent and Merryweather, were already in the front. We could hear them greet our Mom when she walked in.

Bogey pulled the bag of cat treats from our Mom's purse. "Okay, kid. The best time to make our move will probably be around lunchtime. That's when our Mom and Millicent take their lunch breaks. Merryweather will be in charge and she'll have her hands full. Plus that's the time when Nunzio takes his lunch break, too. And he only leaves one employee, Brutus, to run the store."

He passed me a cat treat and took one for himself.

I munched on the treat and nodded. I was trying my very best to remember all I had to remember about this big plan.

Bogey grabbed a couple more treats. "We'll zoom out the door when a customer comes in. We'll have to be really stealthy, kid. We can't risk having someone see us. Otherwise they'll come after us and bring us back."

I nodded. "Got it."

Bogey glanced into the main part of the store. "But first, I think we'd be wise to get some shuteye, kid. We need to be good and alert for this investigation. We'll wake up just before noon."

"Aye, aye," I told him. I was going to salute, but I was just too tired.

Instead I curled up on one of the cat beds our Mom had left at the shop for us. I tried to doze off, but thoughts of burglars and Santa Claus and Christmas cookies just kept floating into my mind.

But I must have dozed off at some point. Because, the next thing I knew, Bogey was shaking me.

"Time to get up, kid," he meowed quietly. "It's almost noon."

With those words, I popped my eyes open and sat up straight. Then I followed Bogey into the main area of the store. That's where we found Millicent and Merryweather talking to our Mom about a big, antique dresser. Millicent had short, curly gray hair and dark-framed glasses that she wore on the end of her nose. She was dressed in a black pantsuit, while Merryweather was dressed in a red polka-dot dress. It matched her red hair and her pretty pink, pointy glasses. Our Mom called them cat-eye glasses. I have to say, I sure liked that name a lot.

Millicent spotted us at once. "Oh, hello, boys," she said. "I didn't know you two came to work today."

Our Mom laughed. "They were pretty determined to get here. But it looks like they just showed up to take a good nap."

Merryweather finished writing out a price tag for the dresser. "That's a cat for you. They'll go out a door, only to want to come right back in again."

Millicent knelt down to pet us. "Would you like me to bring back some leftovers from my lunch? I'm having fried chicken today."

Holy Catnip! She didn't have to ask us twice. Bogey and I rubbed up against her, and I gave her a kiss on the nose. I wanted to let her know that I really, really liked that idea. A lot.

Now our Mom picked us up one at a time and gave us a kiss on the head. "You boys be good. Millicent and I will both be gone for an hour. Merryweather will be keeping an eye on you. I'll be back right after lunch."

I gave my Mom a kiss on the nose, too.

As soon and she and Millicent had left, Merryweather pointed her finger at us. "I know you boys, and I've got a feeling you're up to something. So don't get any ideas of doing something sneaky on my watch."

Neither Bogey nor I so much as meowed in return. Instead we just sat staring at her, purring as loud as we could.

"Uh-huh," Merryweather told us. "Don't think I'm fooled for one minute by that sweet, innocent look. And don't forget, there are cameras all over the store. So I'll be keeping an eye on you two."

Luckily for us, the bell at the front door jingled and a customer walked in. It was a blonde-haired lady wearing a big, fuzzy jacket.

I looked at my brother. "Cameras? She's got cameras?"

Bogey shifted his eyes from one side to the other. "Yup, kid, she does. Our Mom has security cameras to make sure no one comes in and steals stuff. But don't sweat it. Let's just inch our way to the front door."

"Um, okay," I said out of the side of my mouth. "But how? She'll see us."

Bogey ducked down so he was almost flat to the floor. "Just don't make any sudden moves, kid. Nothing that would catch Merryweather's eye. Be stealthy, like I taught you."

"Aye, aye," I whispered back.

I didn't even try to salute, in case Merryweather might see me. Instead I flattened myself out like Bogey did. Then I followed him around the counter and past the place where the cash register was set up.

Next we ran under a settee and a pair of matching chairs. We zigzagged around a camelback sofa and paused behind a bookcase. We ran around that bookcase and then another one. Finally, we passed a few display cases and we were just a few feet from the front door.

That's when Bogey paused. "Let's zoom out the front door when the customer goes out, kid. But we've gotta move fast. We won't have much of a window of opportunity, as they say."

"They do?" I whispered back.

I tried to scrunch down even closer to the floor. But it was kind of hard for a guy my size to get any flatter.

Bogey's tail twitched back and forth, and he put his weight on his back legs. I could tell he was getting ready to leap.

"Yup, kid," he told me. "Now concentrate. We're going to have to spring on outta here."

We could hear Merryweather chatting and laughing with her customer. Then finally, we heard the customer's footsteps moving in our direction, just one row away. Any second now, she'd be approaching the front door and opening it.

From where we were scrunched, we had a clean shot to the front door. All we had to do was wait for the exact right moment to leap and run through when she opened that door.

My heart pounded a million miles an hour. I knew we would be out and on our way to Nunzio's in a matter of minutes.

"Get ready, kid," Bogey whispered to me.

The lady customer had her hand on the door, and we were just about ready to spring.

Then all of a sudden, a pair of high-heeled feet stepped right in front of us. Those feet were attached to a pair of legs. And when I looked up, I saw they were attached to none other than Merryweather.

"Going somewhere, boys?" she asked.

Holy Catnip!

CHAPTER 12

Holy Mackerel!

Bogey and I were caught in the act! How in the world did Merryweather see us? And more importantly, what would she do with us now that we'd been caught? Would she just lock us up in the back so we couldn't get out? Then we'd never have a chance to get to Nunzio's shop!

I suddenly started to shake in my paws. I didn't like getting caught. And I especially didn't like getting in trouble.

I was just about to ask Bogey what to do, when he made his move.

A big, flying leap!

The only thing was, he didn't fly out the door.

Instead, he pounced on a . . . bug?

I blinked to be sure I'd seen it all correctly. And sure enough, he'd leaped right on top of a very, very large bug with wings. Of course, that bug hadn't exactly been moving. Instead, it had mostly just been lying there with its feet sticking up in the air.

Bogey grabbed it in his mouth and ran to Merryweather. Then he promptly dropped that bug at her feet.

Both Merryweather and the lady customer screamed and jumped. They bounced back a few steps, before the customer ran out the door. Merryweather gasped and thunked her hand to her chest. She seemed to be having a hard time breathing.

When she could talk she said, "That's a good, good boy, Bogey. Thank God you killed that awful bug. You're a very good boy. It's cat treats for you guys."

Then she picked us both up and kissed us each on the head. She took us to the cash register counter and lavished us with cat treats.

Bogey grinned the whole way.

I glanced at my brother. I tried to think of something to say, but I wasn't even sure where to start.

"You caught a bug?" I managed to sputter. "A big bug? One that those ladies were scared of?"

Bogey nodded. "Sort of, kid. Sort of. I'm guessing that bug's been dead for a while, kid. It probably just blew in here from the street when someone opened the door."

Now it was my turn to grin. "Oh. But Merryweather and the other lady didn't know that."

Bogey glanced back at the door. "Nope, kid. You might say I was in the right place at the right time. Now let's just keep our eyes open for the *right time* to make our getaway."

I gave him a "paws up."

That "right time" showed up only a few minutes later. That's when a small bus parked directly in front of our Mom's store. Then a whole bunch of ladies trooped out and lined up by the front door. They were wearing nametags and red hats.

When all the women had gotten off the bus, the first one opened the door. "Merry Christmas!" she yelled.

"We're taking a tour of antique stores in three different cities. We're here to shop for Christmas presents."

When the last of the ladies wandered through the door, Bogey and I zoomed out. As near as we could tell, no one had seen us at all. Including Merryweather.

Getting into Nunzio's store turned out to be every bit as easy, too. A customer came out the very second we wanted to run in.

And so we did.

I followed Bogey inside and then we scrunched down low, right next to the front row of shelves. I glanced up for a moment at an entire row of stuffed animals. Just like the ones Gracie had on her bed.

And just like I did at home, I really wanted to snuggle up with those stuffed animals. Because my heart was pounding so hard, I thought it might bounce right out of my chest.

I couldn't stop wondering if we might be in the store with the criminal mastermind we had been trying to catch. The very criminal mastermind who'd been breaking into houses in our neighborhood.

Holy Mackerel!

Bogey pointed to a spot near the end of the shelf unit, so I scooted over with him. From there we had a perfect view of Brutus as he waited on a young woman.

Brutus was tall and had really huge muscles. He had ice-cold, blue eyes and long, golden hair that he kept in a ponytail. Funny, but that ponytail kind of reminded me of the Princess' beautiful tail.

Now Brutus rang up the customer's purchase at the cash register. When he wrote out the receipt for her, he took down her name, address, and phone number, too. Then he gave her the top copy, while the bottom copy stayed in his receipt book. Next he took the lady's money and put the stuff she'd bought into a bag. He handed the bag to her and gave her a smile. She said good-bye and left the store.

But then something very strange happened.

Instead of putting the money into the cash register, Brutus put the money into his pocket. I could hardly believe my eyes.

"Bog . . . " I started to meow. That was, until I felt a skinny black paw cover my mouth.

"Ssshhh, kid," Bogey whispered into my ear. "I saw it, too. Brutus is stealing money from Nunzio's store. The guy's a crook, all right. But let's see what else happens."

Without looking around, Brutus shut the cash register drawer and headed for the back room.

"Here's our chance, kid," Bogey said quietly. "Let's take a look around the store."

So we did. We looked at shelves filled with Christmas ornaments and toys. We saw kitchen appliances and gadgets and pretty drinking glasses. There were T-shirts and tea towels and tablecloths. There were puzzles and games and greeting cards. Row after row, and shelf after shelf, held just about anything anyone could think of to buy.

But nothing looked out of place or out of the ordinary.

When we passed the aisle with the kitchen things, I paused in front of the cookie cutter display. There I saw Christmas Cookie Cutter set #1 and Christmas Cookie Cutter set #2. Just like I'd seen on the receipt I'd found at Mrs. Mitchell's house. The first set had cookie cutters in the shape of Christmas trees and ornaments. It also had holly leaves and snowflakes. The second set had Santa Clauses, angels, bells, and candy canes.

I pointed them out to Bogey.

He nodded to me. "Yup, kid. Mrs. Mitchell shopped here, all right. That was the stuff on her receipt."

Now I felt my eyes go wide. "I wonder if she talked to Brutus or Nunzio?"

Bogey glanced from side to side. "Could be, kid. Could be she mentioned she'd already bought all her Christmas presents. And since Brutus writes down the addresses of the customers, he and Nunzio would know exactly where to go."

I suddenly got the shivers. If Brutus and Nunzio were the crooks, they could have broken into their customers' homes and stolen their presents. Then they could have unwrapped those presents and put the stuff back on the shelves at the store. Since Nunzio already had so much stuff on his shelves, no one would have known the difference!

And that's when it suddenly hit me. Our Mom's store was right next to Nunzio's. What if our Mom came in and told Nunzio and Brutus when she had finished her Christmas shopping? Would they be breaking into our house next?

Holy Catnip!

If I said I was nervous before, well, it didn't even compare to how nervous I felt now! More than anything, I wanted to get out of that store and back to our Mom's store! Right away.

But Bogey motioned me on. "Let's take a listen to what they're saying in the back, kid."

Bogey tiptoed to the edge of the door to the back room. I followed behind him, and together we flattened ourselves against the wall. From where we stood, we had a perfect view of both men as they worked.

Nunzio wasn't as tall as Brutus, but he was every bit as muscular. The two men almost looked like they could be professional wrestlers.

Inside the back room, they were opening and unpacking boxes. The stuff they unpacked looked just like the kind of stuff that Nunzio had on his shelves.

I gasped. "Do you think they're unpacking things they stole from someone's house? Maybe someone's Christmas presents?"

Bogey shook his head. "I don't think so, kid. Look closer. You can see a packing list. That only comes in a box that's been shipped from some company."

Before I could say another word, Brutus suddenly dropped a little wooden jewelry box. It shattered and sent splinters all over the floor.

"Hey," Nunzio said in his deep voice. "Watch what you're doing."

Brutus shrugged. "It's not my fault this stuff is so cheap. It's practically held together with bubblegum."

"You got that right," Nunzio said. "How do you think I make so much money? I sell things that are made with really shoddy craftsmanship. Nothing handmade. This stuff is all put together by some machine. It costs next to nothing to make them and it costs me very little to buy them. Then I sell them for a whole lot more. So I make tons of money."

Brutus laughed. "Don't your customers ever complain?"

Nunzio smiled. "Not really. This time of year, most people are buying them for gifts. And the person who gets the gift isn't going to complain."

Brutus shook his head. "Even if their gift falls apart in a week?"

Now Nunzio laughed. "Nope. Then they'd be insulting the person who gave it to them."

"Sounds like the perfect scheme," Brutus told him.

Nunzio opened another shipping box. "You got that right."

Brutus knelt down to pick up the pieces of the broken jewelry box. Just as he did, he looked out into the main part of the store.

And straight into my eyes.

"There's something in here!" he yelled. "An animal or something. Maybe a really huge rat!"

A rat? Okay, sure I was fuzzy and smaller than Brutus. But I hardly looked like a rat.

"Get it!" Nunzio hollered.

And that's when Bogey and I took off. We raced two rows up and hid behind some shelves. We peeked around the side and spotted Brutus coming after us with a very big board.

"There's two of them," he yelled out to Nunzio.

"I'll get a board and go after them, too," Nunzio yelled back.

"Quick, kid," Bogey meowed to me. "We've got to find a way out of this store."

"But how?" I meowed back.

As far as I could see, there was no way out. We couldn't open that front door by ourselves and no customers had come in for at least a half-hour. We were trapped!

"Head to the front, kid," he meowed. "Around the side of the aisles. Follow me."

Then together we zoomed to the end of the row. We made a sharp turn and then ran straight for the front of the store. Along the way, we zoomed past row after row after row of shelves. My claws dug deep into the hardwood floor as we tore through that huge store. My heart was pumping a million miles an hour, and a cold chill passed over my body as we ran. Even though we were racing at top speed, it seem like the front door was a million miles away. Until now, I hadn't realized how big that store really was.

I could hear Brutus and Nunzio moving up from the back and yelling along the way. They were stomping from aisle to aisle, and hitting their boards along the floor as they went.

"They're trying to smoke us out," Bogey said when we'd reached the final row. The one closest to the door. Ahead was the window that looked out onto the sidewalk.

"Keep moving toward the door," Bogey panted.

I was panting myself as I followed him down that last row. The row filled with stuffed animals.

By now the door was only fifteen feet away. But still no customers had come in so we could run out.

"Jump up into the shelves, kid," Bogey commanded me. "Make like you're one of the stuffed animals. And don't move a muscle."

I did exactly what Bogey told me to do. I jumped up on a shelf and squeezed in behind a stuffed monkey and a stuffed bear. Then I held perfectly still. You might even say I froze into place.

I took a sideways glance at my brother, who had jumped in between a large, green stuffed alligator and a white stuffed kitten.

Then we just stayed really, really quiet. And still. Like statues. Let me tell you, of all the things I've ever had to do as a cat detective, this was by far the hardest. To just sit right out there in the open and stare into space, took every bit of control I had. Especially when my heart was pounding so loud I was sure Nunzio and Brutus would hear me.

Though one thing was for sure — I could hear them. Nunzio was coming around the corner on our left and Brutus was on our right.

Little by little, they inched forward. Right toward us. They were still hitting their sticks on the floor and yelling. By now I could even smell Brutus' breath. And as near as I could tell, he'd had onions for breakfast.

"There's no place to hide, you little rats," Nunzio yelled. "Say your prayers, because you're goners!"

Goners? Did he say "goners"?

Holy Catnip!

CHAPTER 13

Holy Mackerel! By now, Nunzio was just a foot or two away from me. And Brutus was only a few feet from Bogey.

I was so terrified that I started to tremble. But I quickly tensed up my muscles and tried to hold myself perfectly still. Not an easy thing to do when your body wants to shake like a whole tree full of leaves in a windstorm.

Meanwhile, the men inched ever closer. They looked up and down the shelves trying to find us. They both held their boards out, ready to strike.

Then, just when I didn't think I could stand it another minute . . .

It happened. The front door flew wide open and someone walked inside.

Without thinking, I broke out of my frozen statue pose and turned toward the door. Nunzio spotted me just as I recognized the person who had walked in.

It was our Mom!

For once, I didn't have to wait for Bogey to tell me what to do. No, we both pushed off from that shelf and soared through the air. Stuffed animals went flying all over the place, which must have really confused Brutus and Nunzio. Bogey touched the ground once before he jumped into our Mom's arms. And I brushed right past Nunzio and landed on the floor. I made two full-length runs before I was hiding safely behind our Mom's legs.

Our Mom didn't even have a chance to say hello.

Instead she just laughed. "Well, I guess I found you boys. I was pretty worried about you. How in the world did you get over here?"

She reached down and picked me up, too. Bogey and I wrapped our arms around her neck and held on for dear life.

I turned to look at Brutus and Nunzio. They had dropped their boards and were now walking up to our Mom.

"It appears your cats have paid us a visit again," Nunzio said. His mouth was smiling but his eyes weren't.

Our Mom gave him a real smile. "I'm so sorry, Nunzio. I have no idea how they got over here. But don't worry. It won't happen again."

Brutus joined Nunzio. "Lucky for them that you showed up on time."

Our Mom crinkled her brow. "Excuse me? What do you mean by that?"

Nunzio pushed Brutus behind him. "Nothing. He meant nothing at all. Just that a store's a big place. A lot could happen to a cat in a store like this."

For a moment our Mom just stared at him. Then she spoke in a voice that I'd only ever heard her use when she was very, very angry. It was a quiet voice, but whenever she used it, people seemed to listen. And usually backed away.

"If I were you, gentlemen," she said, "I would be much more concerned about me, the cats' Mom, than I would the cats. Because, neither you nor Brutus would want to experience my wrath should any harm come to these animals. I know my friend, Officer Phoebe Smiley, would feel the same way."

She took a step toward the men. "I consider these cats to be part of my family. And I would do almost anything to protect the members of my family."

Nunzio held his hands up. "Sorry, Abigail. Just having a rough day here. You know, with the Christmas rush and all."

Without saying another word, our Mom turned and opened the door. As she carried us out, Bogey and I glanced back at Nunzio and Brutus. Both men stared at us with cold, hard eyes. Stares that made the fur on the back of my neck stand on end.

Our Mom had barely gotten us near her own store when Merryweather jumped out and held the door open for us.

"Well, well, well," she said. "If it isn't Buckley and Bogey. The wayward boys return."

Our Mom just shook her head. "I don't know how, but they managed to get over to Nunzio's."

Merryweather sighed. "I don't know either. They must have gotten out when that busload of ladies showed up. Though I really don't know why they'd want to go over to Nunzio's. He's not exactly an animal lover."

Boy, she could say that again. Not only was Nunzio not an animal lover, but he was a real animal hater! And a guy who could be really scary.

But now I had to wonder, was he was the criminal mastermind who'd been breaking into people's houses? I shuddered at the idea of being home if he broke in.

I cuddled up a little closer to my Mom. She laughed and gave me an extra tight hug.

"I'm going to put you boys in the back," she told us. "I don't want you getting out again. Otherwise you two can't come to the store with me."

Bogey responded to this by purring into her ear. And I gave her a kiss on the nose.

"Okay, boys," she said. "You're forgiven. Why don't you take a nice nap until it's time to go pick up Gracie?"

She didn't have to tell us twice.

We both curled up in our beds.

Bogey pulled out his bag of cat treats. He handed one to me before taking one himself.

He gave me a little salute. "I have to say, kid. You were a real pro back there."

My mouth fell open and my cat treat almost fell out. "I was?"

Holy Mackerel. I sure didn't feel like a pro! I really felt more like a big, giant scaredy-cat.

"Yup, kid, you held it together the whole time. If you hadn't, who knows what might have happened to us?"

I shuddered at the thought. "Do you think Nunzio and Brutus are the ones breaking into the houses?"

Bogey sighed. "I don't know, kid. Could be. We know they're crooks, all right."

I put my paws in front of me and rested my head on my front legs. "I know, I know. We saw Brutus steal money from the cash register."

Bogey nodded. "That's right, kid. And Nunzio is selling lousy merchandise for a big price. He knows that stuff will fall apart right away. But you can bet he doesn't mention that to his customers."

I shook my head. "There are going to be a lot of sad people in St. Gertrude right after Christmas, when their presents all fall apart. Wish we'd learned something that could link Brutus and Nunzio to the break-ins."

Bogey passed us each another cat treat. "I hear you, kid. But the truth is, we didn't find a single piece of evidence that pointed to them being the burglars. Nothing."

I rolled onto my side. "I know. We didn't."

Bogey gave me another treat and took one himself. Then we both just munched quietly for a few minutes. Sure, we'd learned a lot by sneaking over to Nunzio's.

But were we any closer to catching the criminal mastermind than we were before?

Finally, Bogey spoke up. "There is one thing we can do, kid."

My ears shot up. "Oh yeah? What's that?"

Bogey stretched out his front paws. "We can be ready in case they break into our house. We'd better have a plan in place to handle them."

I gulped and almost choked on my cat treat. "Are you kidding me? You saw what almost happened back there! Do you really think we could catch those guys if they ever broke in to our house?"

Now Bogey grinned. "Don't forget, kid. We'd have the advantage. We know the layout of our house. They don't. We can see in the dark. They can't. Plus we could have lots of traps set out for them."

Right about then, I'm sure my eyes went really wide. To tell you the truth, I would have been perfectly happy if I never saw those guys again. Let alone, tried to trap them in our house!

Holy Catnip!

I tried to speak, but all that came out was a bunch of "uh-uh-uh" sounds.

Bogey kept right on grinning. "Glad you're on board with this, kid. We'll talk to Lil tonight and get a plan in place."

And Bogey wasn't kidding. That night, Gracie worked on her cat collars and our Dad worked in his woodshop. Our Mom worked around the house and gathered things our Dad and Gracie would need for the big craft fair on Saturday.

In the meantime, us cats had a meeting.

All of us cats except for the Wise One, of course. At her age, we figured it might be a little tough for her to catch burglars. So Lil and Bogey and the Princess and I all sat in our dining room.

Lil seemed especially happy to help out. She started by asking to borrow Bogey's bag of cat treats. When he passed them to her, she pulled a whole bunch from the bag.

She put three treats in a line with her short white paw. "These treats represent the front door," she told us.

Then she added more treats in more lines. "And this is the hallway and the dining room and our Mom's office."

She continued doing this until she had practically drawn an outline of our whole house. With cat treats! Finally, she and Bogey started talking about something they called "strategies."

Well, right about then, my head started to spin. I'd never heard of something called "strategies" before. But it turned out that strategies were things like, what we could do if burglars broke in the front door. Or what we could do if burglars broke into the back. And on and on.

Before long we talked about things we could use to trip up the burglars. Or scare them, or make them fall on their heads and knock themselves out.

After a few hours, we had come up with an action plan. Bogey and Lil grinned and gave each other "paw bumps" over this plan. But I wasn't so sure about it. My idea was to run away and hide if a burglar showed up. The Princess had agreed with me.

Yet Lil and Bogey were so sure we should take action against any burglars. "A surprise attack," Lil had said several times. And I had to admit, Bogey and Lil had lots of experience when it came to being cat detectives. Since I was barely more than a rookie, I figured they probably knew way more than I did.

So that night, we had action plan drills in between our surveillance runs. And I have to say, it made for a pretty long night. Especially after the day we'd had. Even so, I also had to admit that I was starting to get the hang of the action drill. Eventually I had a pretty good idea what I was supposed to do if a burglar broke in.

Now the question was, would I be brave enough to carry out my part of the action plan if I had to?

Just before morning, Bogey booted up the computer in our Mom's office. I joined him on the desk. While he checked out the local news, I lolled on my side.

The next thing I knew, I heard him make a "tsk, tsk, tsk" sound. "They did it again, kid. There were two more break-ins in St. Gertrude last night."

My eyes popped open wide and I sat up straight. "Really?"

Bogey nodded. "Yup, kid. It looks like our same guys, too."

I gulped. "How can you tell?"

Bogey scooted closer to the computer screen. "Same MO, kid. Same MO."

In case you don't know what MO means, don't sweat it. I didn't used to know what it meant either. But MO is short for Modus Operandi. And the MO is the way a crook operates. Believe it or not, most crooks operate the same way every time. It was one of the first things Bogey had taught me when I became a cat detective.

I moved over to look at the computer screen. "Did they take the Christmas presents again?"

Bogey rubbed his eyes with his sleek, black paw. "Yup, kid. They took them all."

"And the wreath on the front door?" I asked.

"You got it, kid," he answered me. "And here's the interesting thing. In one house they took the star ornaments off the tree. Even the star on the top."

I gasped. "Just like at the Nelsons'!"

He flexed his right front paw. "That's right, kid. And in the other house, they took the star off the top of the tree and the bright star from their indoor manger scene. Plus they took the star candle holders, the star Christmas placemats and the lighted star decorations from the windows."

"Wow," was all I could breathe. "These crooks sure do like stars!"

Bogey grinned at me. "You've got it, kid. They like stars, all right. I'm guessing it's their weakness."

I looked right at Bogey. "Their weakness?"

Bogey nodded. "Yup, kid. Every crook has a weakness. And it looks like our crooks can't resist taking these stars."

"Wow," I said again. "Is that important?"

Bogey turned off the computer. "You bet it is, kid. It might be the clue that leads us right to them."

Holy Catnip!

CHAPTER 14

Holy Mackerel! The rest of the week went by in one big blur. Our humans spent every extra minute of their days getting ready for the Craft Fair. And us cats spent every minute of our nights running surveillance and action drills.

Of course, Bogey checked the local news each day, too. And each day he read more reports of more break-ins. All of the break-ins sounded pretty much the same. With presents, wreaths, and stars stolen from each house.

By now all the citizens of St. Gertrude were on edge. The police were stumped. No matter how hard they tried, they couldn't figure out who was committing these crimes.

Even so, the big craft fair was still on for Saturday as scheduled. So on late Friday afternoon, Gracie packed up the hundred or more cat collars she had made. She put them in a big cardboard box, along with a pretty red tablecloth and the sign for her booth.

I sat on the kitchen chair next to her and watched.

She smiled and petted me on the head. "I sure hope I sell most of these, Buckley. I worked really hard making all these collars. I want to make enough money to buy Christmas presents for the whole family. Plus, I saw the prettiest winter coat in a store downtown. I am just dying to get it. So will you be a good boy and help me sell my collars?"

I stood on all fours and purred up to her. Then I gave her a nice, wet kiss on her elbow. Of course I planned to help her. I knew she'd worked really hard, night after night. And I wanted to make sure all her hard work paid off.

She was just finishing up when our Dad walked in. He had a huge grin on his face.

"This might help," he told us.

Then he set a little red sleigh on the floor. One that he had made himself. One that had wheels and a harness. So I guess you could say it was more of a wagon, even though it looked like a sleigh.

"Here you go, big guy," he said as he picked me up.

The next thing I knew, he had placed me in that harness.

He scratched me behind my ears. "You can pull this around while you're wearing one of Gracie's collars. That'll have everyone buying Gracie's collars *and* my Christmas lawn ornaments, too."

Holy Catnip! At first I wasn't really sure what to think about the whole idea. But then I figured, hey, if it helped out my family, well, I was in!

Before I could take a single step, Bogey came trotting into the room. He jumped into the back of the wagon and grinned at me.

"Let's see if you can pull this thing, kid," he meowed.

"Hang on," I told him.

Then I shifted my weight forward and started to pull. The wagon rolled right along behind me, just as slick as silk. Our Mom walked in just in time to see me pull that wagon across the kitchen.

I could hardly believe the way our humans acted when they saw me. Our Mom and Dad and Gracie all cheered and laughed!   I guess it made them pretty happy to see me pull my wagon with Bogey riding.

Minutes later our family went back to packing things up for the show. I ducked out of the harness and then practiced getting back into it again. Before long, I was pretty good at getting that harness on and off.

After dinner that night, our humans headed to the St. Gertrude Events Center to set up their booths.

Bogey and I stayed behind and kept an eye on things at our house.

Bogey passed me a cat treat. "It's going to be a big day tomorrow, kid."

I glanced out the window. "I know. I wish I was looking forward to it."

Bogey grinned. "You never know, kid. It might be perfect for our investigation. Our burglars could be there, too."

That's when I'm sure my eyes went wider than ever before. "The burglars? Going to a craft show? Do you really think so?"

"Yup, kid," Bogey told me. "St. Gertrude is a small town. And everyone goes to this craft fair. Let's keep our eyes peeled for someone who has lots of stars to sell. Or maybe someone who is buying lots of stars. You know how our burglar can't keep his paws off the stars."

"Wow," I breathed. "You're right. I never dreamed we might run into our burglars there. Do you think Brutus and Nunzio will go?"

Bogey grabbed a treat from the bag. "I'd count on it, kid. Nunzio will be there to check out the competition."

I raised one eyebrow. "Competition?"

Bogey nodded. "Yup, kid. The stuff sold at the Craft Fair will be good quality. Because it's homemade. Not like the junk that Nunzio sells."

I munched on a treat and glanced out the window again. Up until that moment, I really hadn't thought much about the Craft Fair. Now it seemed like it could be important to our case. And it sounded like we'd be doing a whole lot more than just selling cat collars!

Holy Mackerel!

Before I could say another word, the doorbell rang.

Ding-dong!

Bogey's ears went up and I stood at attention. Of course, us cats couldn't answer the door. But we certainly wanted to know who was there.

I was about to run and glance out the front window when Bogey held up his paw.

"Hold on there, kid. Something doesn't feel right," he said quietly. "It's Friday night and our Mom and Dad aren't expecting anyone. Best not to take any chances. Let's holler at Lil and get into action plan positions."

But we didn't even need to call Lil. Instead she showed up at the office door with the Princess right behind her. The Princess' eyes were huge, and I could tell she was pretty scared.

"Everybody ready?" Lil asked in her most serious voice. "Detective Bogart? Detective Buckley? Princess Alexandra? All in?"

We stood in a circle and Lil reached a paw into the middle of the group. Bogey did the same but put his paw on top of hers. Then I reached my paw in and put it on top of Bogey's. The Princess looked from side to side and scrunched up her face. I could tell she wasn't sure what to do at the moment.

I leaned over and whispered in her ear. "Stack your paw on top of the rest of them."

The Princess nodded. "Oh, okay. Thank you, Buckley."

She licked her paw a few times until it was good and clean. Then she did as I told her to. She put that wet paw right on top of mine.

Bogey and Lil both blinked a few times. But nobody said a word because the doorbell rang again.

Ding-dong! Ding-dong!

"Positions!" Lil commanded. "Front door positions!"

And we all scurried to our spots.

Bogey nodded to Lil. "I'm going to take a glance outside. See if I can tell who's here."

Lil nodded back. "We've got you covered."

Then Bogey slinked across the hardwood floor, just as low as he could get. He didn't make a sound.

I'd never seen a cat be as stealthy as Bogey was right at that moment.

He lifted his head up at the bottom of the curtain. "I can't tell who it is. It's dark out and it looks like they're wearing black. I think there's two of 'em. The porch light is off."

"Oh, no!" I gasped. "Our Mom and Dad must have forgotten to turn it on before they left!"

"Looks like our drills are about to pay off," Lil said in a low voice. "Everyone ready?"

"Ready," we meowed back.

Now the people outside started knocking on the door. Pounding actually. For a moment there, I thought they might even break down our front door.

It was almost as loud as the pounding of my heart.

Then everything went silent.

Every piece of fur along my back stood on end. The suspense was almost more than I could stand. I glanced over at the Princess. Her eyes were bigger than I'd ever seen before, and she was shaking like she was cold.

All the while I had to wonder, had the people left? Or were they just getting ready to make their next move?

Then we all heard it. Voices outside. They were so low we could barely pick them up.

And all of a sudden, Bogey waved his paw and motioned for us to move. "Back door! They're heading for the back door!"

"Change of plans," Lil hollered. "Take your back door action plan positions!"

I have to say, I've never seen a group of cats move so fast. In a matter of seconds, we had shifted gears and we were ready for a break-in at the back door. I guess Lil and Bogey had been right, making us practice our drills over and over.

Because even with my heart pounding and my nerves frazzled, I could still do the job I was supposed to do.

But then I heard a noise I didn't mind hearing at all. Our Dad's truck turning into the driveway. His headlights brightened up the whole night.

I glanced at Bogey and Lil and the Princess. Relief was written all over their furry faces. Everyone sighed "whew" at almost the same time.

A few minutes later, I heard our Mom's voice. "Mike and Mesmeralda! So nice to see you."

"Hello, Abigail," Mrs. Mitchell's voice said. "We just wanted to return your casserole dish. Nobody answered the front door, so I was going to leave it at the back. I didn't want anyone to steal it. I thought the back door would be a safer place to leave it."

"Well, thank you," our Mom said.

Bogey let out a deep sigh. "False alarm, everyone. It was only the Mitchells."

Lil nodded to each of us. "That's okay. It was good practice for us all. Good job, team! You make me proud to be a feline."

The Princess finally smiled. "I've never been part of a team before. I like it. It feels so nice."

I smiled at her just as the door from the garage opened up. Our Mom and Mrs. Mitchell walked inside.

Our Mom took the casserole dish from Mrs. Mitchell. "Is your booth all set up for the Craft Fair tomorrow, Mesmeralda?"

"We're all ready," Mrs. Mitchell said. "I hope we sell lots and lots of wreaths. So we can pay for new Christmas presents."

Our Mom put the dish into the cupboard. "I'm sure you will, Mesmeralda."

Mrs. Mitchell glanced around the room. "My, but you certainly have done lots of decorating for Christmas. You look like you're all ready for the holiday."

"Amazingly, I am," our Mom laughed. "I just need to wrap my presents, bake a few cookies, and pick up a turkey for dinner."

Did she say turkey? Right at that moment, my mouth began to water. Just the thought of turkey made me hungry. I had my first taste of it over Thanksgiving, and let me tell you — it tasted good! I could hardly wait to eat it again.

Mrs. Mitchell stared at her feet. "I wish I could be as organized as you are, Abigail. But ever since the break-in, I just can't seem to get focused."

Right then, Gracie bounced into the room. "Why don't you come to my Christmas play, Mrs. Mitchell? That will cheer you up!"

For once, Mrs. Mitchell smiled. "Well, dear, I think that is a splendid idea. When is your play?"

Gracie smiled back. "It's next Friday night. At seven thirty."

"We'll be there," Mrs. Mitchell answered. "But now I'd better get home. Mike and I will have a big day tomorrow. We've got to get our rest."

"We'll all need our rest," our Mom laughed. Then she walked Mrs. Mitchell outside.

That was when I flopped over onto my side. I closed my eyes and dreamed about eating turkey.

In fact, I was almost sure I could smell turkey. But how could that be? Our Mom wasn't cooking turkey yet.

I opened one eye to see Bogey standing over me. He was waving a cat treat in front of my nose.

"Turkey-flavored cat treats," he said with a grin. "This'll get you going for a while. Because we have a long night ahead of us, kid."

Holy Catnip.

CHAPTER 15

Holy Mackerel! The next morning, it was still dark out when our Mom and Gracie put Bogey and me in our pet carriers. We waved good-bye to Lil and the Princess as we were being carted out. Bogey and I hated leaving them short-pawed for the day, especially with so many break-ins going on around town. And especially when we knew it would be pretty hard to put our action plan into place with just the two of them.

But we had no choice. Bogey and I had to go help our family at the Craft Fair. And that was that.

Suddenly I felt just a little bit nervous. After all, I'd never been to a craft fair before. I glanced out the window and watched as we passed lots of houses. I noticed other people had lawn ornaments up, too. And lots of people had wreaths on their doors and Christmas lights along their rooflines. I had to say, St. Gertrude sure looked pretty for the Christmas season.

The St. Gertrude Events Center was also decorated for Christmas. Two tall trees sparkled with lights at the front entrance. And a big sign adorned with a giant-sized bow announced the Craft Fair today. On the inside, garlands and ornaments were strung up all over the place. Strands of lights twinkled from the ceiling to the floor. And there were five big trees in the entryway, all decked out in different decorating themes.

It was enough to make a guy's head spin. Especially when Gracie carried me into the area with the booths. Although, most of the booths weren't actually booths at all. Instead they were just areas that had been sectioned off, side by side, down a row, on opposite sides of the aisle. And they all looked completely different. But most of them had tables or shelves, so the people could display the stuff they'd made to sell. Some people had curtain backdrops, and almost everyone had a sign.

These "booths" stretched as far as the eye could see. There were rows and rows and rows of them. And they filled the whole Events Center.

And let me tell you, even though the Craft Fair wasn't officially open for business yet, the place was hopping! There were so many sights and sounds and smells that I could barely take it all in. I smelled everything from cinnamon to pine trees to nutmeg. Bells were ringing and Christmas carols rang out through the loudspeaker. A group of Christmas carolers in old-fashioned clothing practiced in one corner.

As we passed each booth, I saw that people were selling just about *anything* and *everything* that had *something* to do with Christmas. There were handmade ornaments and flower arrangements. There were placemats and cookies and cakes. There were hand-knitted sweaters, hand-painted bow ties, and quilted tree skirts. And on and on and on. Most of it in green, red, gold or silver. The colors were all so vivid that I didn't know where to look first.

Holy Catnip!

In front of me, our Mom carried Bogey in his pet carrier.

"Keep your eyes peeled, kid," he meowed back to me. "Things are going to get real busy real quick. So better take a good look around before the place fills up with people."

"Aye, aye," I meowed back. I tried to salute him but I only ended up falling on my side. Let me tell you, trying to keep your balance inside a pet carrier can be a big challenge.

Still, I got back up again and glanced out. I remembered what Bogey had said about the crooks having a weakness for stars. So I tried to spot all the stars that I could.

Pretty soon I realized that almost everyone had stars at their booths! Even Gracie had put stars on her cat Christmas collars. And our Dad had made some big wooden stars covered in lights that people could hang on their roofs.

I shook my head and covered my eyes with my arm. How would we ever spot a crook who liked stars in a place like this? With so many stars on display?

I took a deep breath and peeked again.

And that's when I saw it. The brightest star in the whole Events Center. Several rows away, someone had put a big, huge star high up on a really tall pole. The star was so big you might even say it was gigantic. That star could be seen everywhere.

Something told me it would be a good place to start looking for clues.

If we could ever figure out how to get there.

After going over a few aisles and then down an entire row, we finally arrived at Gracie's booth. And I had to say, I thought her booth was the prettiest of all. She had her shiny red tablecloth across her table, and the cat collars looked so colorful hanging on their display stands. Plus she'd made a curtain for the back of her booth from some kind of shiny, glittery fabric. She had a big sign pinned to the fabric that read: "Dress your Cat up for Christmas, Too. With Cat Christmas Collars."

She'd even brought a stand for Bogey and me to sit on while we helped with the sales.

And that's exactly where we were sitting when the doors opened and the people all came in to shop.

Before they arrived at our booth, Gracie slipped a bright, green satin collar with a white bow tie on me. And our Mom put a red collar on Bogey. His had little gold and green ornaments attached.

I have to say, we looked kind of handsome in those collars. Bogey gave me a "paw bump" just before a whole pack of people arrived at our booth.

"What are these?" one lady asked.

"Cat Christmas collars," Gracie told her.

"Okay, kid," Bogey meowed. "Here's your chance. Put on your 'cute' routine."

And so I did. I remembered everything Lil had taught me, just before we went undercover in a cat show once.

I tilted my head to the right.

"Ohhhh, how cute," one lady sighed.

Then I tilted my head to the left and raised my right paw. This brought "oooohs" and "aaahhs" from the crowd.

Then all of a sudden, everyone wanted to buy one of Gracie's collars. In fact, the more I tilted my head and looked cute, the more collars she sold. Our Mom took the money and made change, while Gracie put the collars in bags for her customers.

Bogey grinned at me and stretched out on the stand. "Good job, kid. I think you've got the hang of this."

With a big yawn, he just sat back and enjoyed the show.

Two hours later, Gracie had so many sales that she couldn't help but squeal. "You're doing great, Buckley. I've already made enough money to buy Christmas presents! Keep up the good work!"

She kissed me on the top of my head.

So I kept on tilting my head back and forth and raising my paws. I looked just as "cute" as I possibly could.

There was only one problem with the whole plan — after a while, I started to feel really, really dizzy.

All at once I noticed the room seemed to be spinning.

I heard Bogey say, "Deep breaths, kid. Deep breaths."

But by then it was too late. I couldn't tell which way was up or which way was down. And suddenly I felt myself falling, falling, falling.

Right into the box with the extra cat collars.

"Buckley!" Gracie hollered. "Are you okay? Did you get hurt?"

I waited until my eyes straightened out again. Then I crawled up the side of the box. I had collars draped on both of my ears and several along each arm. I even had one in my mouth.

I spit it out and hung onto the edge of the box.

Gracie brushed off the collars and picked me up. Then she held me tight.

"I'm going to get an extra special present for you this year," she said. "You've been such a big help to me."

Our Mom petted me on top of my head. "Maybe the boys need a little break. Why don't you put them in their wagon and take them for a little walk? You can put some collars in the back and sell them along the way."

"Sounds good, Mom. Could I please have my money so I can go Christmas shopping?"

"Sure, honey," our Mom said. "I'll take care of things here at your booth while you're gone. Be sure to stop at your Dad's booth and see how he's doing. Don't be gone too long."

Gracie pulled our red wagon out from under her table and put it in front of her booth. Then she put me in the harness and Bogey in the back. She grabbed a whole bunch of collars and put them all around Bogey.

"I won't be long at all, Mom," she promised.

And we were off. Gracie walked beside us as I pulled Bogey in the wagon. We'd only gone a few feet when someone noticed us.

"Ooooohhh," a lady with curly black hair said. "That is the most adorable thing I've ever seen!"

And the next thing I knew, the crowd sort of parted to let us go past. Almost like we were in a parade.

"What are you selling?" an older gentleman asked.

"Cat Christmas collars," Gracie said with a smile. "Just like my cats Buckley and Bogey are wearing. I made them myself."

The man smiled at her. "I'll take three."

A young woman jumped in, too. "I'll take two for my cats."

And that was how it went. I pulled Bogey in the wagon and the crowd scooted out of the way for us. Gracie sold more and more collars as we moved along.

At the rate she was selling cat collars, I figured she'd be able to pay for college before long.

Finally, after what felt like an hour, we arrived at our Dad's booth.

He laughed when he saw us. "You boys are really earning your keep today!"

Bogey barely had a chance to meow back before someone asked about our wagon that looked like a sleigh. And the next thing we knew, our Dad started selling wagons and other lawn ornaments, too.

Finally, Gracie waved good-bye to him. "I'm taking Buckley and Bogey and going Christmas shopping, Dad!"

"Spend wisely," he told her.

So we kept on rolling up the aisle. About halfway up, Gracie stopped and bought a beautiful emerald-green sweater for our Mom. Then we moved up a few more booths and she bought some barbecue mitts and a barbecue apron for our Dad.

She wrapped her gifts in tissue paper and hid them in the bottom of our wagon. That's because she wanted our Mom and Dad to be surprised when they opened their presents on Christmas Day. Of course, we were more than happy to help her with that surprise.

Once she had her presents stowed away, we rolled on again. We passed a few more booths, and then Gracie spotted a necklace she thought her friend might like. So she stopped to buy it for a Christmas gift.

That's when I pointed to the big star in the middle of the store. "Take a look up there," I told Bogey. "I'll bet our crooks would absolutely go crazy over that star."

Bogey grinned at me. "I'll bet you're right, kid. And I'll bet there are even more stars in the booth below it. Let's go check it out."

I turned to look at my brother. "But how? Gracie's almost finished with her Christmas shopping. She'll be ready to go back to her booth in a few minutes."

Bogey grinned. "Not if we lead the way, kid. Not if we lead the way."

I looked up and down our aisle. "But how will we find it? I'm kind of lost already and I don't know what row it's in."

"Don't sweat it, kid," he told me. "Just follow the star. It'll lead us there."

I crinkled up my brow. Hmmmm . . . where had I heard that before? Wasn't it part of the Christmas story the Wise One had told me?

I started pulling the wagon again and led the way, just like Bogey had told me to do. And sure enough, Gracie followed behind. As she did, she sold even more collars and bought more presents.

A few minutes later, I came to the end of the row and turned left. All the while I kept that star in my sights. Of course, it wasn't exactly easy to do. Not with all the tall humans who wanted to stop and pet us. Or buy a collar from Gracie.

Still, I pulled that wagon on and on, until I found the right row. Then I took another left and headed down toward the booth with the big star.

Right about then, I started to feel a little tired. Pulling our wagon had been fun at first. But now I only wanted to get out of that harness, flop over, and take a break.

But I knew I couldn't take a break right at that moment. And I knew Bogey wasn't big enough to pull the wagon himself. If I stopped now, Gracie might take us all back to her booth. Then we'd never have a chance to check out that star.

Well, let me tell you, when I signed up to be a cat detective, Bogey told me there would be times like this. So I took a deep breath and pushed on. We had to check out that booth, no matter what. For all I knew, we might find the clue that could crack this case wide open. Or . . . at least break it open a little bit.

And I sure didn't want to miss that.

Behind me, Bogey must have figured out that I was getting kind of tired. So he jumped down from the wagon to lighten the load.

He handed me a cat treat. "Here you go, kid. This'll keep you going."

I munched on the treat and leaned forward once more. Bogey walked beside me as I rolled on. My muscles ached and my feet hurt a little bit, too. But I just focused my eyes on that big, bright star.

We were about halfway down the aisle when we finally spotted the booth right below that star.

Actually it was three booths. They'd all been taken up by one business. And what a business it was!

Suddenly my heart skipped a beat. "Bogey, I think I'm seeing stars . . ."

Bogey gasped. "You got that right, kid. I think you hit the mother lode!"

My jaw fell open so far I thought it was going to hit the floor. For a second or two, it felt like I couldn't even breathe.

For there before us, at the St. Gertrude Craft Fair, was the biggest collection of stars I had ever seen in my life.

Holy Mackerel!

CHAPTER 16

Holy Catnip! I could hardly believe my eyes. For a few moments, all I could do was sit and stare at the triple-wide booth. I looked from star to star to star to star. I don't think I'd ever seen so many stars in one place before. Except for in the night sky when Bogey and I gazed out the window.

There were star ornaments, star candleholders, star wall hangings, and star furniture. There were star nightlights and star mobiles. I saw stars covered in lights, stars covered in rhinestones, and stars covered in glitter. Right in the middle of it all was an entire display of stars for the top of Christmas trees.

Just about every kind of star a cat could imagine was right there inside that booth.

Eventually, all those stars turned into one big blur in front of my eyes. So I shook my head and tried to refocus my sight.

Then I glanced up at the sign on the top that read: "Starry, Starry Night, Inc."

I gulped. "Wow, how will we ever find some clues in all this stuff? It could take us days to go through all this."

Bogey jumped back into the wagon. "Don't sweat it, kid. We'll just cut through the muck."

I glanced from side to side. "The muck?"

To tell you the truth, I didn't exactly see a lot of muck. So far, all I could see were a whole lot of stars.

I was about to ask Bogey what he had in mind, when the lady who ran the booth noticed us.

She squealed so loud we both kind of jumped. Then she slapped her hands to her cheeks and stared at us with her mouth wide open. She had a huge head of golden hair that stuck out in points everywhere. Her blue eyes looked giant-sized behind her big, black-framed glasses that were covered with little rhinestone stars. Plus she had star rings on her fingers and a shirt with a big star on it.

"That is the cutest thing!" she shouted. "Hello, kitties!"

Before we could so much as meow, she waved to Gracie. "Hello, there! Are these your cats? They're adorable. My name is Star Gazer and this is my booth. Could I interest you in a star for Christmas?"

Gracie's eyes went wide and she kind of choked for a moment. "You sure do have a lot of stars."

"Yes, we do," Star said. "And you sure have some handsome cats. What are you selling?"

Gracie smiled at Bogey and me. "Cat Christmas collars. Would you like to buy one?"

"Ooooh," Star said. "I've got a beautiful gray cat named Orion. And a beautiful striped tabby named Cassiopeia. They'd love some Christmas collars. Would you be willing to trade me for some?"

Gracie's eyebrows went up. "Trade?"

"Sure," Star answered. "You give me some cat collars and I'll give you some stars in exchange. Do you see anything you'd like?"

Gracie pointed to a set of three glass star ornaments. They had shiny gold flecks inside the glass.

"I like those," Gracie said. "They would look beautiful on our Christmas tree."

"It's a deal," Star told her. "Now, I'll take two of those red collars and two gold collars in exchange."

Gracie handed the collars to Star, and Star pulled the ornament set from the display. Then she passed the set to the huge, hulking blond man next to her. He was kind of hunched over and didn't look at us at all. He started wrapping Gracie's star set in tissue paper.

Now Star smiled with bright, white teeth. "This is my boyfriend. His name is Big Dipper. Say 'hello,' Big Dipper."

But the man didn't really speak and only kind of grunted at us.

"Nice to meet you, Mr. Dipper," Gracie told him. "And you, too, Miss Gazer. My name is Gracie and these are two of my cats. Buckley is the big one and Bogey is the shiny one."

"Nice to meet all of you," Star said.

But her boyfriend still didn't say a word.

"Are you finished with your Christmas shopping?" Star asked.

Gracie smiled up at her. "I just finished a few minutes ago."

"Good for you!" Star twinkled at us. "Say, haven't I seen you around before? Aren't you Abby's daughter? The lady who owns Abigail's Antiques?"

While Gracie and Star talked away, Bogey jumped down and nudged me in the ribs. "I'm going in, kid."

I glanced from one side to the other. "In? In where?"

Bogey grinned at me. "In there, kid. I'm going into the booth to take a look around. If there's a clue in there, I plan to find it. You stay here and cover me."

I gulped. "Um, okay. But how are you going to get in?"

Bogey tiptoed over to the edge of the booth. "It's easy, kid. There's nothing but a tablecloth here. I'll sneak right under and go poke around. You keep them distracted by looking cute."

I rolled my eyes. There was that word again. Cute. Why did I always have to be the one who looked cute?

I knew what Bogey would say to that. It was all part of the job. Anyway, let me tell you, I put on my cute routine, all right. I tilted my head right. Then I tilted my head left. But for once, it seemed like nobody noticed me.

And if nobody noticed me, that meant they might notice what Bogey was up to instead.

Holy Mackerel!

I knew I had to do a better job of getting people's attention. Our case might depend on it! I thought for a few seconds and figured I might have more luck if I moved to a higher spot. And the best way for me to get to a higher spot was to have Gracie hold me.

So I slipped out of my harness and slid in next to her. I circled her legs and rubbed up against her. Usually she picked me up when I rubbed around her legs. But this time she didn't pay any attention to me at all. She was too busy talking to Star.

Then I remembered what Bogey had told me. That desperate times call for desperate measures. That's when I stood up on my hind legs and stretched my front legs up to Gracie's waist. I tipped my claws in ever so slightly, just enough so she couldn't ignore me. Without glancing down, she picked me up and held me in her arms.

I was all ready to go back into my cute routine, but I decided to take a good look around first. After all, if Bogey was looking for clues below the booth, I knew I should probably look for clues above.

I had barely focused in on the middle table when I spotted a slim black paw reaching up from behind. Then I saw sharp claws come out and latch onto the receipt book. Seconds later, that receipt book disappeared from the top of the table.

I knew exactly where it had gone. Bogey had it beneath the table and he was checking out the receipts.

Now I really had to keep the humans distracted so he had a chance to investigate!

Holy Catnip!

I was about to start tilting my head from side to side when I saw someone waving to Gracie.

"Hello, dear," said Mrs. Mitchell. "I see you've traded for some stars."

I turned to see that the Mitchells had the booth right next to Star's three booths. And they had tons of beautiful Christmas wreaths for sale.

Gracie smiled and waved back. "How are you doing, Mrs. Mitchell? Are you selling lots of wreaths?"

Mrs. Mitchell smiled. "We've been doing very well. I've sold so many wreaths I can't keep track of them all. I think we'll be able to afford new Christmas presents now."

"I'm glad," Gracie said. "I've almost sold all of my cat Christmas collars. And I did all my Christmas shopping here today."

"Good for you," Mrs. Mitchell said. Then she stared right at me. "I see you brought your cats with you again."

Gracie gave me a hug. "I couldn't have done it without them. But wait a minute, where is Bogey?"

As soon as she said his name, his head popped out from under the tablecloth in front of Star's booth.

Gracie leaned over to put me back in my harness.

Above us, I heard Star turn to chat with Mrs. Mitchell. "Mesmeralda, I'd love to get one of your wreaths. Would you be willing to trade me for something in return?"

But Mrs. Mitchell didn't exactly sound very excited. "Uh, I guess. Okay," she said.

Star, on the other hand, sounded very excited. "What would you like? Just name it."

"Well," Mrs. Mitchell said slowly. "I like kitchen things. Things to bake with. Do you have any cookie cutters? And I like Christmas ornaments."

"I've got them all," Star laughed.

She handed Mrs. Mitchell three different star cookie cutters and two star ornaments. Then Star selected the biggest, most brightly decorated Christmas wreath on Mrs. Mitchell's table.

"But, wait . . ." Mrs. Mitchell started to say. Then she just clenched her teeth and set her jaw in a firm line instead.

Gracie put Bogey back into the wagon. "Come on, boys! We've been gone for too long. Mom is probably wondering where we are by now."

And that was that. We were off. Gracie waved good-bye to Star and Mrs. Mitchell. Star was smiling and Mrs. Mitchell looked kind of sad. And Big Dipper just kept his head bent and his eyes on his work.

I didn't have a chance to talk to Bogey until we were halfway back to Gracie's booth.

"What did you find out?" I meowed.

"Something pretty interesting, kid," Bogey meowed back. "You'll never guess whose name was in that receipt book."

Well, he had me there. I could probably never guess the name, no matter how hard I tried.

"Who?" I called behind me.

"Nunzio," Bogey told me.

I stopped dead in my tracks. "Nunzio? Nunzio bought stuff from Star? When he can get stuff at his own store?"

"Yup, kid," Bogey said. "But like we said, he probably wanted to get some good stuff. Not the junk he sells at his store. But here's the clincher. Turns out Nunzio likes stars."

I glanced back at my brother. "He does? How could you tell?"

Bogey leaned closer to me. "Because, kid, he bought a lot of stars."

I choked for a moment. "He did?"

"Oh yeah, kid," Bogey said. "He bought star ornaments and a Christmas tree topper. He bought lighted stars for the windows. And he bought star-shaped candles. He bought a star tie and cufflinks. And a lighted star that rotates in circles. He even bought a toothbrush with a star on the end."

"Wow," I breathed. "He really does like stars. A lot."

"You got it, kid," Bogey agreed.

I started to pull the wagon again. Then I came to the end of the row and turned left.

"What else did you find out?" I asked. "Did you recognize any other names in the receipt book?"

Bogey leaned into the turn. "Nope, kid. No other names stood out. But Star didn't write down the names of the people who traded stuff with her. She only wrote down the names of people who paid for things."

"That's true," I said. "She didn't. And she sure wanted to make lots of trades."

I could hear Bogey munching on a cat treat. "But she probably only traded with people here at the Craft Fair. And so far, we haven't spotted anyone else here who looks suspicious."

I looked ahead and spotted the row where Gracie's booth was located. "And we've been down most of the rows. We saw most of the booths."

"I hear you, kid," Bogey said. "We did. But there is one other thing."

I paused for a moment to let Gracie sell some more collars.

"What's that?" I asked Bogey.

He handed me a cat treat. "Did you notice anything about that Big Dipper guy? Did he look familiar to you?"

I thought about it for a minute. To tell you the truth, I didn't really get a good look the guy, since he never looked me in the eye. But from what I saw, I realized he did look kind of familiar. Like I'd seen him somewhere before. But where?

I nodded to my brother. "He does remind me of someone. I'm just not sure who."

Bogey grinned. "How about Brutus, kid? Does he remind you of Brutus?"

And that's when I realized he did. In fact, if Big Dipper had looked me in the eye, he could have been Brutus' twin.

My mouth fell open and I looked at Bogey. "Do you think they're . . ."

"Brothers?" Bogey finished my sentence for me. "That's my guess, kid."

"And do you think they might be . . ." I started.

"Working together?" Bogey finished again. "It wouldn't surprise me a bit, kid. Then again, nothing in this business surprises me anymore."

I remembered what we'd seen in Nunzio's store. "Brutus was already stealing from Nunzio. He took money from the cash register."

Bogey looked from side to side. "Don't I know it, kid. Don't I know it."

Gracie finished up her sale, and I went back to pulling the wagon. By now I could see Gracie's booth again. Our Mom smiled and waved at us.

Gracie smiled back. When we got to the booth, Gracie shook her finger and told our Mom not to look in the bottom of the wagon. Because that's where Gracie had stashed all the Christmas presents she'd bought. With her back to our Mom, she put Bogey and me on our stands. Then she hid the wagon under her table.

Our Mom laughed and gave us all a kiss on the head.

I responded by giving my Mom a kiss on the nose.

Yet all the while, I couldn't stop thinking about what Bogey had said. Was it possible that Brutus and Big

Dipper were brothers?   Could they be the criminal masterminds who were breaking into people's houses?

Maybe Brutus found out the names of people who had finished their Christmas shopping while he worked at Nunzio's store.   Then he and Big Dipper could have broken into those people's houses later.

But somehow I had a hard time picturing either Brutus or Big Dipper as being criminal masterminds. Okay, sure, I could see them as criminals, all right.   But masterminds?   That was the part I was having trouble with.   They just didn't seem like the type of guys who could break in, steal stuff and not leave a trace behind.

I shook my head and sighed.   Were Bogey and I getting any closer to solving this case?

Sometimes the cat detective business could really make a guy's head spin!

Even so, I had to admit, we had uncovered a lot of pieces to the puzzle.   But now the question was, how would we make all those pieces fit into one big picture?

Holy Catnip!

CHAPTER 17

Holy Mackerel! The rest of the Craft Fair went by in a big whirlwind of happy people and Christmas things. Bogey and I stayed on top of our stands and helped Gracie sell the last of her cat Christmas collars. But we also kept our eyes peeled for anyone who might look suspicious. Yet as hard as we tried to spot anyone out of place, nobody stood out to us at all.

Even so, I was happy to see Gracie looking so pleased. She'd made enough money to buy Christmas presents, plus the coat she'd seen in the store window downtown. So I guess you could say it was a pretty successful day.

When it was all over, our Dad joined us and helped Gracie and our Mom pack up.

"Did you sell lots of lawn ornaments?" Gracie asked our Dad.

"I sold a bunch," he told her. "But I didn't sell as much as you did."

Gracie smiled at us. "That's because I had Buckley and Bogey here to help me."

Our Mom smiled, too. "They were a big help. That's for sure."

An hour later, we were resting in our pet carriers while our humans finished packing up their booths. Then we headed home, but our Dad took a detour through a fast food drive-up window. He ordered hamburgers and fries for the humans and chicken patties for us cats.

Once we got home, we were all so tired we could barely keep our eyes open. I was almost too tired to eat dinner. But I got through it and somehow managed to enjoy every bite of my chicken.

Right after dinner, Bogey dragged himself to a cat bed and flopped down. Let me tell you, his eyes were shut and he was fast asleep in a matter of minutes. Maybe even seconds!

Holy Catnip!

Then Gracie went to the sunroom to practice her lines for the Christmas play. I guess she wanted to rehearse her part in front of the Wise One. Somehow I figured Miss Mokie would really enjoy the chance to see Gracie's performance.

In the meantime, our Mom went to her office to count the money they'd made at the Craft Fair. And our Dad started to unpack all the things from our booths that he'd loaded in his truck. He'd parked his truck in the driveway, and I watched him from the dining room window.

Funny, I was so tired and yet I just couldn't stop thinking about all the things I'd seen today. My head practically swam with images of Christmas stuff. I remembered seeing a million different ornaments and Christmas trees. Not to mention, all the stars and lights and bows and garland. The odd thing was, all that Christmas stuff made me feel really warm and happy inside.

But why? I still wasn't sure if I understood the real meaning of Christmas. And why so many people wanted to celebrate it.

Just then I saw our Dad take my little red wagon out of the back of his truck. He set it on the lawn while he unloaded more boxes and display things from the show.

The sight of my wagon made me smile. And I was dying to run around with it one more time. That way I could remember all the wonderful times we'd had today.

Would it really hurt if I sneaked out for a few minutes to see my wagon?

After all, Bogey and I had gone outside once before. We came right back in and everything had been just fine.

So I figured it would be okay if I went out while our Dad was still working. As long as I got back inside before he finished unpacking his truck.

I trotted to the door in the kitchen that led to the garage. And when my Dad walked in, carrying an armful of boxes, I zoomed out beneath his feet. I was sure he hadn't even seen me.

Now all I had to do was sneak in the same way I'd sneaked out. It would be so easy.

I ran through the garage and out onto the driveway. My Dad had the garage door open while he was unloading his truck. So there was nothing in the way to stop me.

Outside it was dark and chilly. Except for the streetlights and our porch light. But being a Maine Coon Cat, the chill and the darkness didn't bother me.

At least not at first.

I trotted down the driveway until I saw my wagon on the grass. The sight of it made me smile all over again. Especially when I remembered pulling it around the Craft Fair while Gracie sold her cat collars.

I ducked under the harness and began to tow my wagon, just like I did before. It was a little rough going down the driveway, but as soon as I hit the sidewalk it rolled along nice and smooth.

Then I pulled my wagon over to look at the Nativity scene in our front yard. It was the first time I'd seen our yard completely decorated. Or, rather, it was the first time I'd seen it from the front, anyway.

I got out of my harness and crouched on the grass. Then I watched the twinkling lights as they ran up and down the strands — all the way from the grass to the star attached to our roof. And I looked at baby Jesus in the manger. Along with his Mom and Dad. Mary and Joseph. The whole scene was lit up with a spotlight. And I had to say, baby Jesus looked pretty peaceful just lying there on his little bed of straw.

The whole yard was so bright and pretty and magical. I just stared for a long time. It seemed like I couldn't look away. But I knew it was time for me to go back inside the house. So I got in my harness and started to take the wagon back to the garage.

I was almost to the garage door when I noticed something was different. The garage door was down! And my Dad's truck was locked up. To top it off, my Dad was nowhere to be seen!

I could hardly believe it! I had waited too long to go back inside my house.

Holy Mackerel!

I was locked outside!

All of a sudden, I started to shake a little bit. I had never been locked out before. And more than anything, I wanted to be inside my house with my family. I wanted to be sharing cat treats with Bogey and getting hugs from Gracie.

Instead, I was a cat out in the cold.

Tears pooled in my eyes and rolled down my cheeks. I missed my family and I missed my home. I missed my Christmas tree and I missed my food dish. And yet I was only a few feet away from it all.

To make things worse, I knew there were probably burglars out running around, too. What if they found me outside? I remembered how Brutus and Nunzio had gone after Bogey and me with boards. If those guys were the burglars and they tried to get me, well, I would be in trouble. Big trouble. My family would never even know what happened to me.

More tears ran down my cheeks and I tried to wipe my eyes with my big paw. But I missed and hit myself in the nose instead.

For some strange reason, this made me laugh. I don't know why, but it did.

The minute I laughed, I quit crying. And I realized I had to pull myself together. I had to be brave and figure out what to do about my situation. After all, I was a cat detective. Cat detectives didn't go around crying just because they'd been locked out.

No, good cat detectives were like Bogey and Lil. They didn't get scared. They used their heads and thought of ways to solve the problem!

It was exactly what I had to do, too. So I scrunched down for a moment and tried to think. Then I glanced up at our front porch, and I remembered when Hector had gotten locked out. He'd gotten our attention so we could help him get back inside his house. Surely I could do the same. Plus, I would probably be missed before too long. After all, Bogey would be starting the surveillance rounds pretty soon. He'd know right then and there that I was gone.

Still, I didn't exactly want to wait until it was time for us to run surveillance. Instead, I wanted to let Bogey know right away that I was outside. So I pulled the wagon to the side of the house, just below the kitchen window. Then I stood in the wagon and reached up to the window. And let me tell you, I'm a big guy and very tall when I'm stretched out. But I still wasn't tall enough to look over that window ledge. I could touch it with my paw, but that was about as far as I got.

That's when I realized that all the windows in our house were that high up. All the windows except for the dining room windows, that is. And they came almost down to the floor. If I had hopes of getting anyone's attention, it would have to be from there.

So I hid my wagon behind a shrub to make sure it would be safe from any burglars. Then I ran around to the front porch and to the dining room windows. I tried to look in, but the curtains were already drawn. Worse yet, it looked like my family had gone to bed early! Probably because they were so worn out.

Still, I knew if I could get a cat's attention, they might peek their head out. And see me.

But to get their attention, I knew I had to make some noise. A lot of noise. So I started meowing. Really loud. And I scratched on the window. Then I tried what Hector had done and even I bumped against the window. I kept on meowing and scratching and bumping, and let me tell you, I was one cat who made quite a racket!

Holy Catnip!

I kept on making a racket until, finally, I saw a small, white head lift up the bottom of the curtain. Big, green eyes stared out at me. As always, my heart started to thump really loud. It was the Princess. I was always happy to see the Princess, but tonight, I was especially happy. I guess you could say she was a sight for sore eyes. Or rather, "cold" eyes.

Her little mouth dropped wide open. "Buckley! Buckley! Are you okay? What are you doing outside?"

"I got locked out," I told her. "It's kind of a long story. I'll explain it all later. Can you go tell Bogey I need help?"

She nodded her head. "Sure, Buckley. But Bogey is asleep. I guess he was really worn out after today. He hasn't even started surveillance yet. Or the action plan drills."

I crouched down on the wooden porch. "Please wake him up, Princess. And tell him I'm locked out. Tell him I need him to help me like we helped Hector."

The Princess crinkled her brow. "Huh?"

I shivered in the cold air. "Don't worry. He'll know what I'm talking about."

"Um, okay, Buckley," she said. "I'll go tell him."

And with those words, she scampered off. I knew that once she told Bogey, he'd figure out a way to wake up the humans and get them to open the door.

Now I just had to wait until he managed to get me back inside the house.

The temperature outside had dropped a bunch and I huddled on the porch to keep warm. From where I was hunched, I could see the Nativity scene and baby Jesus lying in his manger. I wondered if He was feeling kind of cold, too.

So I jumped off the porch and ran to the manger. Then I crawled on top of the straw and cuddled up next to baby Jesus. Just like the cat in the story the Wise One had told me. Funny, but as I tried to warm up baby Jesus, I could have sworn I was the one getting warm.

I glanced over at his Mom, and I thought I saw her smile. Then I looked up at the night sky, for the brightest star out there. A million stars twinkled back at me, but one or two stood out as being really brilliant. I tried to imagine what it must have been like all those years ago. When that bright star in the sky led people to where Jesus had been born. What a beautiful night it must have been.

Almost like tonight was.

And somehow, even though I was locked outside, I smiled inside.

I was enjoying the sight of the night sky, when I heard someone calling my name.

"Buckley! Buckley!" Gracie's cries pierced the night.

I jumped up and made a beeline straight for her. Then I leaped into her arms just as she leaned over to pick me up. She hugged me so tight that I couldn't even move.

"Buckley," she cried over and over again. "I can't believe you got locked out. Do you know how sad I would be if I lost you? Oh, Buckley, it would have ruined my life forever."

She kept on hugging me as she brought me inside the house. My Dad was there, too, in his bathrobe.

"How in the world did you get out, big guy?" He scratched my ears.

I gave him a kiss on the nose. Then I glanced around my house. I was home. I was back with my family. And I couldn't remember ever feeling happier.

That night Gracie took me up to bed with her. She kept her arms wrapped tightly around me. She held on to me for a long, long time and wouldn't let me go.

Bogey popped his head in once or twice while he was running surveillance. "Welcome back, kid. I want to hear all about it when you're free."

I gave him a "paws up."

Later, when I was able to sneak out of Gracie's arms, I made my first upstairs surveillance run of the night. As always, I found the Wise One on her purple velvet sofa in the sunroom.

I bowed and she waved me on in. "Ah, young Detective. Princess Alexandra has informed me of your recent adventures. Sounds as though you've been having an interesting time as of late."

She could say that again.

I nodded to her. "Yes, ma'am. I sure have."

She waved her paw above me. "I can also see that you have questions on your mind. Something is troubling you."

It was? Holy Catnip. *Here we go again.* I wasn't really aware of anything that was bothering me. Except for all the usual stuff. But when I thought about it, I guess there was one thing I wanted to ask her about.

I sat back and looked up at her. "I don't understand. Who was Jesus and why do we celebrate Christmas?"

The Wise One paused for a moment. "Ah, yes, young Detective, I can see where this might all be confusing. But I believe you'll find the answers in this ancient text. It has been copied onto this sheet." She pointed to a bunch of papers that had been stapled together.

I recognized them as the script for Gracie's play.

The Wise One hooked a claw into the papers and pulled them closer to her. "These words of wisdom were also once part of a wonderful Christmas television program. The words rang as true then as they do now."

I scooted closer and hunched down on the floor, with my paws before me. "What does it say?"

The Wise One cleared her throat and began to read. "Now there were in the same country shepherds living out in the fields, keeping watch over their flock by night. And behold, an angel of the Lord stood before them, and the glory of the Lord shone around them, and they were greatly afraid. Then the angel said to them, 'Do not be afraid, for behold, I bring you good tidings of great joy which will be to all people. For there is born to you this day in the city of David a Savior, who is Christ the Lord. And this will be the sign to you: You will find a Babe wrapped in swaddling cloths, lying in a manger.'"

Miss Mokie took a deep breath before reading on. "And suddenly there was with the angel a multitude of the heavenly host praising God and saying: 'Glory to God in the highest, And on earth peace, goodwill toward men!'"

The Wise One looked up at me and pushed Gracie's script back to where it had been. "Those words, young one, should give you the answer to your questions. Then you'll understand the real meaning of Christmas."

"I will?" I breathed.

For once, Miss Mokie smiled. "Yes, you will. You have done well, Grasshopper. But now I must rest."

"Thank you, Miss Mokie," I whispered as she closed her eyes.

I quietly tiptoed around the room and checked all the doors and windows. I didn't make a sound because I didn't want to wake her.

Yet the words she had spoken rang through my mind. Before long, you might say the light began to dawn, and I finally started to understand what Christmas was all about.

And though I sure enjoyed all the pretty trees and lights and ornaments and everything else, it was nice to know the meaning behind Christmas. It really was a birthday party.

And what a birthday party it was!

Holy Catnip.

CHAPTER 18

Holy Mackerel! The next week flew by so fast I could barely remember it all. As usual, we ran surveillance and action plan drills at night. Gracie practiced her part in the Christmas play right after school every day. Our Mom worked late at her antique store all week since she had so many Christmas sales. And our Dad took over the dinner duty.

Presents that were wrapped in colorful paper and tied with bows showed up under our Christmas tree. On Wednesday, I helped Gracie wrap the presents she had bought for our Mom and Dad. Then she put them under the tree with the rest of the pretty packages.

I figured it was also time for me to think about the presents I wanted to give to everyone. So I decided to take Bogey's advice about giving something I might like, too. I went to my stash of cat toys and picked out some of my favorites. I found a pretty white mouse for the Princess, and a super high-bouncing ball for Bogey. I grabbed a cuddly stuffed animal for Gracie and a pretty feather toy for our Mom. And so on and so on. Until I'd picked out presents for everyone. Since I didn't know how to wrap my presents, I just took them to the tree. Then I hid them against the wall, right behind the biggest present there.

I stopped for a second and just stared at our tree. A big smile crept across my face, and suddenly I felt like I was glowing all over with happiness. Maybe it was the spirit of Christmas that the Wise One had told me about. Because giving all those presents really did make me feel happy.

I looked up to see Bogey stroll in and park himself beside the tree.

"Got your presents stashed under here, kid?" he asked me.

I kept on smiling. "Uh-huh. Something for everyone."

He grinned. "Feels kind of nice, huh, kid?"

"Oh yeah," I told him. "But you know, Bogey, I've been thinking . . ." I started to say. Then I stopped. Because I wasn't quite sure how to say what I wanted to say.

Bogey put his paw on my shoulder. "Go ahead, kid. Spit it out. Come on. You can do it!"

"Okay," I said. Then I took a deep breath and went on. "It's like this. When I was at the cat shelter, I didn't know anything about Christmas. And we didn't have presents. The cats that are still there won't be getting any presents. Plus, I don't think Santa ever visited the place either."

Bogey shook his head. "Wow, kid. That's a tough break. Talk about a sob story. Santa must not know about the place or he would've shown up."

I nodded. "That's what I figured."

Bogey stretched out his front feet. "But it sounds like you've got a plan brewing in your brain, kid."

"Well," I said slowly. "We don't play with all of our toys. Maybe we could give some of them to the cats at the shelter. Then they'll have Christmas presents, too."

Bogey grinned at me again. "I like it, kid. I like it. Have you thought about how we'd get those toys to them?"

"Remember our wagon?" I asked him.

My brother nodded. "How could I forget, kid?"

I sat up nice and tall. "Well, on the night I got locked outside, I hid it behind a shrub."

"Good job, kid!" Bogey cheered. "We could cart all the toys to the shelter in our wagon. The shelter's only a few blocks away."

I stood up and started to pace. "Uh-huh, that's what I was thinking. But first we'll have to figure out a way to get us and the presents outside."

Bogey shook his head. "Don't sweat it, kid. We'll get Lil and the Princess in on it. Together we'll come up with a plan."

Now it seemed like I couldn't stop smiling. "Plus, maybe we can tell Santa about the cat shelter, too. And make sure he goes over there."

"Good idea, kid," Bogey said. "Even if we don't see the big guy, we can leave him a note."

That's when I stopped smiling. "What do you mean, if we don't see him?"

Bogey licked his front foot. "Santa's quick, kid. He's in and out of here in a hurry. After all, he's got lots of places to deliver presents to in one night."

Suddenly my chest felt a little heavy. "Wow, I sure hope I get to see Santa."

Bogey shook his head. "You never can tell, kid. Some cats get to see him and some don't. If you blink, you'll miss him. Our Mom will leave milk and cookies for the big guy. That'll slow him down for a second or two. But after that, he's outta here."

"Wow," I sighed.

It was funny how Santa went into people's houses and left presents. Whereas the Christmas Crooks, as they'd been called by our local newspaper, went in and stole presents. Yet somehow I guessed Santa was probably a really happy guy, since he gave away so many presents and made everyone else happy.

But the Christmas Crooks probably weren't happy at all, even though they stole stuff for themselves. And they, in turn, made others unhappy. It was strange how it worked that way.

I shook my head. Sometimes all this giving and taking stuff could be confusing. But there was one thing that wasn't confusing to me at all. I knew I'd rather be the kind of cat who gave more than he took. I'd rather make others happy.

Bogey had been keeping track of the latest news on the Christmas Crooks. Every night we'd read more reports of the burglars breaking in to houses around St. Gertrude. At the rate they were going, pretty soon no one would have any Christmas presents at all. Soon the whole town would be unhappy.

Thankfully the Christmas Crooks hadn't hit our house.

Not yet, anyway.

I kept that in mind as we ran our action plan drills every night. I was happy that our family had been safe from the crooks so far.

Especially when I knew that Gracie had other things on her mind anyway. She'd been practicing her role in the play so much that I don't know how she could even see straight. By the time Friday night rolled around, I could tell she was a little bit nervous about it all. She was dressed up in her angel costume, and wow, did she ever look beautiful! She could barely eat her dinner, and she just kept saying her lines over and over again.

Us cats, on the other paw, didn't have any problem eating our tuna fish dinner. And let me tell you, we sure enjoyed her performance! With our plates on the floor near the kitchen table, we heard every word that Gracie said. We knew she'd be wonderful in the play.

But I wasn't so sure that *she* knew that. So I gave her an extra kiss on the nose before she left, just to let her know.

It was dark outside and the porch light was on when our humans left for Gracie's play. I watched them in our Dad's truck as he backed it down the driveway and drove off. More than anything, I wished I was going with them. I wanted to see Gracie up on the stage when it was all decorated and lit up.

I was feeling kind of sad when the Princess came to sit beside me. As always, my heart started to thunk really, really loud.

She leaned her little head on my shoulder. "You miss her already, don't you, Buckley?"

I rested my head on top of hers. "I wanted to see her in the play. I'll bet she does a really good job."

"Me, too," the Princess purred.

For a few moments, we just sat there like that. It was so nice and peaceful. And it sure made me feel a whole lot better. Together we stared out at the Christmas lights in the front yard. Our Dad had left all the lights off in the house, so the outdoor lights would stand out even more.

And let me tell you, they stood out, all right. They twinkled and ran up and down the strands. I kept on staring, and I couldn't look away even if I wanted to.

Then all of a sudden it seemed like my heart was pounding a whole lot louder than usual. Sure, I always had a big reaction when I was around the Princess. But this time my reaction sounded ten times louder than it normally did.

That's when I realized the pounding wasn't coming from my heart at all. Instead, it was coming from the front door.

Holy Catnip!

Whoever was out there pounded again. Even harder this time. Then I saw the light go out on the front porch. Seconds later, I heard a *crunch* outside.

"They smashed the light bulb," Bogey said.

I realized he'd come up behind us. His eyes were huge and his ears were leaning straight forward. I could tell his senses were on *full alert.*

I felt my eyes go wide. "They did what?"

Bogey spoke faster than I'd ever heard him talk before. "They took the light bulb out and broke it. To keep it dark."

I crinkled my brow. "Why would they want it to be dark? People can't see . . ."

And before I'd even finished my sentence, I knew exactly what Bogey was saying.

Especially after I saw our beautiful front porch wreath come flying through the air and land by the window.

I gasped and so did the Princess.

"Positions!" Bogey commanded. "This is not a drill! This is the real deal! Front door positions now!"

The real deal. The words rang through my head as I took my position. *The real deal.* Someone was about to break into our house. The Christmas Crooks had been breaking into houses all around town. And now they were here at ours.

My heart felt like it was in my throat and I could barely breathe. Would it be Brutus and Nunzio at our door? Or Big Dipper and Star Gazer? Or Brutus and Big Dipper, the two men we suspected were really brothers?

I grabbed a strand of Christmas lights that we had hidden behind the potted palm.

Lil came rushing into the room. "Are we ready?"

"Ready!" I hollered. Exactly like I did during our drills.

"Ready," squeaked the Princess.

"I was born ready," Bogey said.

We didn't have time to gather in a group and put our paws into a circle this time. Sure, it would have been a real boost for us if we did. But we knew couldn't waste even a second.

"They're wearing black," Bogey announced as he peeked out the curtain. "There's two of them."

Now the pounding stopped and I heard thumping footsteps moving across the front porch. That meant the burglars were on the move and headed to the . . .

"Back door positions!" Lil commanded. "Hurry!"

We all scrambled just as fast as we could from the front of the house and into the kitchen. Then we took our back door positions. The Princess jumped high atop the cabinets, right next to the heavy ceramic cookie jar. Lil and I crouched in front of the cat food plates on the floor.

By now we could hear a fumbling noise at the back door. A small beam of light shined into the room.

"I see a flashlight," Lil yelled. "Bogey, are you ready?"

"I'm on it!" was his response as he leaped up onto the kitchen table.

If I didn't know better, I would have said that Bogey was almost enjoying himself. Right at that moment, I would have given anything to be even half as brave as he was. Because, let me tell you, I was anything *but* brave! My paws were shaking and every piece of fur on my back and tail stood at attention. With my fur sticking out, I looked like I was three times my real size.

I only hoped my larger than normal size might make me look kind of scary!

But I didn't get much time to think about it. Not after the glass in the back-door window suddenly shattered.

I gasped.

The burglars had broken in! The Christmas Crooks were here!

Holy Mackerel!

I saw a black-gloved hand reach inside. It turned the doorknob and unlocked the door.

My heart skipped a beat when the door flew wide open. Seconds later, two people dressed in black stepped into our kitchen. They had on black ski masks so I couldn't see their faces. One was a lot bigger than the other, and they kept the beam of their small flashlight aimed at the floor. Probably so it couldn't be seen by anyone driving by our house.

The two burglars moved silently into the kitchen.

"Got it, Bogey?" Lil meowed.

"Got it," he hollered back, just before he crouched into a springing position.

He shifted his weight back and forth on his hind legs once or twice. Then he pushed off and catapulted himself into the air. He came down on the wrist of the bigger burglar who'd been holding the flashlight. I knew Bogey had his sharp claws fully extended when he made that surprise attack.

The burglar screamed and dropped the flashlight. Lil was already racing across the floor before that flashlight even hit the ground. When it did, she batted it from side to side with her front paws, like she was hitting a soccer ball. The little flashlight went spinning into the family room. In a matter of seconds, she had it hidden way under the couch.

The bigger burglar leaned over and grabbed his wrist. "What was that?"

"Maybe they have a parrot," whispered the other burglar.

"I don't know," said the first one. "But let's get the stuff and get out of here! Fast."

For a second, I thought I kind of recognized those voices. But I couldn't quite put faces with the voices.

"You're up, Buckley," Lil meowed to me.

So I went into position. I jumped up onto the counter, right behind the smaller burglar. I got a running start and I leaped right onto that crook's back. I had my claws full out and I dug in hard when I landed.

"Eeeooooow!" screamed the smaller burglar. That burglar fell forward and started to stumble around the room.

I even managed to get in a bite through the ski mask, onto the burglar's neck. Then I sprung off, touched on the countertop, and leaped onto the floor.

By then Bogey and Lil were back in position.

The little burglar was still screaming and the bigger burglar looked like he was trying to help.

"Plates!" Lil yelled.

When the smaller burglar moved forward, Lil sent one of our cat food plates sliding across the floor. Lil's aim was perfect and the plate hit its mark. It went right beneath the smaller burglar's foot as the crook stepped forward. The burglar's foot went down on top of the plate and that person went sliding across the floor, almost landing in a splits position. That burglar let out quite a scream. Then Bogey sent another plate flying that tripped up the big burglar.

"It's those cats!" the smaller burglar yelled. "Those cats are doing this to us. Get 'em!"

That's when I pulled my strand of Christmas lights out from behind the cabinet. Bogey took one end of the strand and I held on to the other. Then Lil picked up the partly smooshed jingle bell collar that we'd hidden behind the potted palm. She waved it in the air to get the burglars' attention.

And to get them to run toward her.

As she did, Bogey and I ran in opposite directions with the light strand ends in our mouths.

I heard that familiar "jingle, jingle, jingle" of the collar as the burglars ran straight for Lil. Bogey and I pulled our strand tight about a foot off the floor, just in time to trip the burglars.

The little burglar went down again with a *thud*, and the bigger burglar tripped and landed right on top of the smaller one. The little burglar cried out, and the bigger burglar fell over and hit his head on the floor.

In a flash, Bogey made a beeline to the computer in our Mom's office. That's where he had it all set up to dial 9-1-1 by computer and send a message to the police.

The burglars moaned and rolled around on the floor. In the meantime, the Princess went into action. She pushed and pushed just as hard as she could against that huge cookie jar on the top of the cabinets.

"A little to the left," I coached her.

"Now give it all you've got," Lil hollered.

Let me tell you, I've never seen that little Princess try so hard as she did right then. She scooted back and then ran at that cookie jar for all she was worth. She hit it with her shoulder and put all her weight into it. She did her very best to shove it off the ledge, but she was just too tiny.

The heavy ceramic cookie jar barely budged an inch. In that instant, I realized we were short on muscle and short on time. Clearly the Princess needed some help.

It was one of the few times in my life when it paid to be an extra large cat.

I soared onto the counter, then leaped up on the refrigerator and finally to the top of the cabinets. Then I zoomed over to the cookie jar.

Just as the burglars were getting to their feet!

I didn't have a second to lose. So I got into place, right behind that heavy cookie jar, all ready to push it over the ledge.

That's when it hit me.

Cookies.

Suddenly, all the things we'd seen and investigated about this case came flooding back into my mind. That's when all the pieces of the puzzle fell into place.

I knew who the Christmas Crooks really were.

And I had to say, considering the way they'd had everyone fooled, they truly were criminal masterminds.

Holy Mackerel!

CHAPTER 19

Holy Catnip!

More than ever before, I knew I had to stop the Christmas Crooks who were rolling around on the floor below me. Otherwise, no one would ever believe they were the people behind the break-ins. They had hidden their true identities so well all along. If I didn't stop them now, they might just get away with their crimes. And worse yet, they might just keep on stealing from everyone in town!

As far as I was concerned, they'd done enough damage to St. Gertrude. Worst of all, they'd tried to ruin Christmas. For everyone.

When Bogey first told me about Christmas, he told me it was the best. Little by little, I'd learned that he was right. Now I still wanted it to be the best for Bogey and my family, and for me, too. And the rest of St. Gertrude.

But for that to happen, I needed to end the crime spree of the very crooks who were on our kitchen floor.

So I took a deep breath and tried to shove the big, giant cookie jar with all my strength. And that's when I finally understood why the Princess couldn't push it off.

I could barely make it move myself and I was about four times her size. I guess we hadn't realized this was one cookie jar that weighed a ton!

By now the burglars were starting to get to their feet.

That meant I had to push the cookie jar off the ledge, and I had to push it off fast.

"Come on, Princess," I ordered. "This is going to take both of us. We've got to do this together."

She nodded her little chin. "Okay, Buckley. Whatever you say."

We both took a few steps back and got a running start. We aimed straight for that cookie jar and gave it everything we had. Together we hit it with such force that the cookie jar slid almost halfway off. Then we gave it one more shove and the huge thing finally tipped over the edge.

And it went falling, falling, falling . . .

Right smack-dab on top of the little burglar's head.

It landed with a loud *whuuuump* that echoed around the kitchen. Then the cookie jar bounced to the floor without even breaking into pieces. I could hardly believe it.

The little burglar went down in a heap. For a moment, she just lay on the floor. Not making a sound. And not moving. I guessed we had probably knocked her out cold.

Sirens wailed in the distance, which meant Bogey had gotten through to the police.

The bigger burglar began to slap the smaller one in the face. "Mesmeralda!" he said over and over. "Wake up! Wake up! We've got to get out of here!"

He tried to pick her up but he slipped on one of the food plates we had on the floor.

He went down again but quickly pulled himself up. He picked Mrs. Mitchell up a second time and tried to make his way to the door. I jumped down from the top of the cabinets and onto the counter.

By now Bogey was back, and he intercepted Mr. Mitchell as he tried to escape. He bit him on the back of the leg and Mr. Mitchell fell forward again. He dropped Mrs. Mitchell and fell on top of her once more.

I jumped onto the floor just as Mr. Mitchell managed to grab his wife and throw her over his shoulder.

"Jingle bell collar, kid!" Bogey hollered to me.

And I knew exactly what he was talking about. I ran and grabbed that collar from Lil and made a beeline to the back door.

Bogey bit Mr. Mitchell on the other leg. Just as he went down again, I dropped the collar into Mrs. Mitchell's pocket.

The sirens sounded even louder, and Mr. Mitchell picked up his wife once more and headed out the door. He stumbled along and kind of zigzagged out into the back yard.

He ran around the garage and hid in the shadows. Bogey and I followed behind him.

"They're getting away!" I hollered.

Police cars pulled up, and their flashing lights lit up the neighborhood. Officer Smiley and a few other officers were heading to our front door.

"Jump on his back, kid. We've got to get the Mitchells out where people can see 'em," Bogey commanded.

So I did just that. I jumped onto Mr. Mitchell's back with my claws fully extended. And let me tell you, I dug in deep! Mr. Mitchell let out such a shriek that I'm pretty sure people heard it from three blocks away.

With my final attack, Mr. Mitchell ran down the driveway. He carried his wife, and my jingle bell collar in her pocket went "jingle, jingle, jingle" all the way. They made such a ruckus that the police couldn't help but notice them. The police all turned and aimed their flashlights at the Mitchells. Mr. Mitchell dropped to his knees and pulled off his ski mask. Then he pulled off his wife's.

"We were attacked," he screamed. "It was those burglars!"

Just then our Mom and Dad and Gracie pulled up. They came running out of the car to tend to the Mitchells.

Officer Smiley ran over to help them, too.

"Oh no!" I meowed. "Everyone thinks the Mitchells are victims! They don't know the Mitchells were the crooks!"

But much to my surprise, Bogey just sat back on his haunches and grinned.

"We've got to stop them," I hollered at my brother. "We've got to do something.

"Don't sweat it, kid," he said with an even bigger grin. "I'm way ahead of you on this one."

Right about then, my jaw fell open wide and I could hardly speak. I wondered if my brother had been hit on the head, too. Or had he been injured in the scuffle? Because I could hardly believe what he was saying. Didn't he want to stop the Christmas Crooks?

Before I could take a good look at him and make sure he was all right, another young officer came running up into the yard.

He waved at Officer Smiley. "Phoebe, you're going to want to see this. We just got a pretty interesting email."

He held his cell phone out so Officer Smiley could read it.

She read the email and her eyes got so big I was afraid they'd pop out of her head! Then she turned red and looked so mad I thought steam was going to burst out of her ears.

She almost sort of growled and pointed a finger at the Mitchells. "Cuff Mr. Mitchell and take him to the station. Take Mrs. Mitchell to the hospital first, and when she's better, we'll put her in jail, too."

"But wait," Mr. Mitchell sputtered. "You can't do that! We're the victims here."

"Don't even start with me," Officer Smiley said. "You had us all fooled but now we know better. It wasn't nice to ruin Christmas for the good people of St. Gertrude."

Mr. Mitchell leaned back on the lawn and glared at everyone. "You can't prove a thing."

A smug smile came over Officer Smiley's face. "Oh yes we can. It's all right here in this email. Somebody mapped it out for us quite nicely. Every clue and all the pieces leading up to solving this crime."

Mr. Mitchell scowled. "Where did that email come from?"

"You can worry about that in jail," Officer Smiley said.

I gasped and looked at my brother.

He only grinned in return.

I grinned back at him. "You figured it out, too!"

He nodded. "You got it, kid."

I crouched down and looked out into the yard. "And you sent the police an email."

He nodded. "With all the details and clues that we'd already found, kid. Leading the police right to the Mitchells' door."

"When did you know?" I asked him.

I was amazed when Bogey pushed a fake rock out of the way and came up with a bag of cat treats.

He pulled the pouch open wide. "Right after I knocked the flashlight out of Mrs. Mitchell's hand, kid. I caught her scent. Then all the pieces added up and made sense."

He handed me a cat treat. "How about you, kid? When did you figure it out?"

I munched on the turkey-flavored treat. "When I looked at the cookie jar. That made me think of cookies and I remembered Mrs. Mitchell's cookies. She said her 'star cookies' had all been stolen. But when we found those cookie cutter sets at Nunzio's store, there were no star cookie cutters. She traded for some at the Craft

Fair. So she didn't have any star cookies. So no star cookies were ever stolen."

Bogey popped a cat treat in his mouth. "You got it, kid. Plus the star was never stolen from the top of her Christmas tree. But the stars were stolen at every house that was broken into. So I'll bet Mrs. Mitchell has a real thing for stars. She must have worked pretty hard to make sure her booth was right next to the Starry, Starry Night booth at the Craft Fair."

I grabbed another treat from the bag. "That's where she was selling all those Christmas wreaths. Wreaths that she had stolen and just decorated differently. I'll bet she made a bundle selling all those."

Bogey patted me on the back. "Good job, kid. Good job."

I smiled. "Thanks. You, too."

Now Bogey grinned bigger than I'd ever seen him grin before. "You know, kid. You're turning into a first-rate detective."

And that was when I couldn't say even one more word. Funny, but I felt all choked up inside. I liked the idea of being a first-rate detective. If I got to be as good as Bogey was, well, I'd be one very happy Maine Coon cat.

I turned to my brother and best friend, Bogey. Then I tried to salute him. And this time, well . . . I got it just right.

Holy Mackerel.

By now an ambulance had arrived and was taking Mrs. Mitchell away on a stretcher. She was starting to come to, and rolling her head around a little. She just kept saying, over and over again, "Those cats . . . Those cats . . ."

Officer Smiley turned to another officer. "Wake up the Judge and let's get a Search Warrant. I'll bet our missing presents are right there inside the Mitchells' house."

Later that night, no matter how many times we told the story, we all enjoyed it every time. Bogey and Lil and the Princess and I all gathered in the dining room.

The police were outside our house and in our kitchen, finishing up all the crime scene stuff. And judging from the flashing lights down the street, I guessed they were working at the Mitchells' house, too.

"There's one thing I don't understand," the Princess said. "I thought Mrs. Mitchell was a victim of the crooks. How could the Mitchells be victims and the burglars at the same time?"

Bogey grinned. "That was part of their plan. As criminal masterminds. They only made it look like they'd been victims."

I nodded. "To throw everyone off their trail. Because nobody would ever suspect people they believed were victims of the burglars."

Now Lil jumped in. "And, as you'll recall, they were the *first* victims. So from that time on, they knew nobody would ever dream they might be the crooks."

"Oh," the Princess nodded her little head. "So they were sort of hiding out as victims, in a way. That's pretty smart, I guess."

Bogey passed us a round of cat treats. "They threw us off the trail when they went over to the Nelsons' house. They were there the night Bogey and I went to check things out."

I chomped on my treat. "Of course, when we smelled their scent, we thought it was from their visit that night. We didn't know their scent was also there from the break-in."

"You got it, kid," Bogey said. "You got it."

We were just munching on some more treats when Officer Smiley and our Mom walked into the room.

Officer Smiley gave our Mom a hug. "Thanks to that email you sent, Abby, we have enough evidence to put the Mitchells away. For a long, long time."

Our Mom raised one eyebrow. "Email? I didn't send you an email, Phoebe. We were all at Gracie's play this evening."

Officer Smiley looked at her cell phone. "But the email was sent from your computer."

Our Mom looked over at the phone. "What name is on it?

"It says BBCDA," Officer Smiley said.

Our Mom rubbed her head and blinked a few times. "What in the world . . .?"

For a second, both our Mom and Officer Smiley turned and looked at Bogey and me.

"Could it be . . .?" our Mom started to say.

But she finished her own sentence with, "No, it's not possible . . . is it?"

Bogey and I just purred and smiled up at her. It wasn't her fault that she didn't know what BBCDA stood for. The Buckley and Bogey Cat Detective Agency.

Holy Catnip.

CHAPTER 20

Holy Mackerel! After Bogey and I caught the Christmas Crooks, the rest of the days leading up to Christmas were really happy ones. People kept stopping by and bringing Christmas cookies and presents. Some people even brought cat treats. A bunch of Christmas carolers came to the door one night and sang songs to us. And Christmas lights sparkled on all the lawns in our neighborhood.

Except for at the Mitchells' house, of course.

All in all, it was a pretty wonderful time of year.

Then, at long last, Christmas Eve rolled around. I was so excited to see Santa for the first time in my life, I could hardly stand it.

Our humans went to church right after dinner. Then they came home and went straight to bed. I guess they were pretty worn out from all the Christmas activities. In the meantime, us cats stayed up to see the big guy in the red suit.

But first, Bogey and I had a little Christmas Eve gift-giving trip of our own to make. We had to deliver cat toys to the cat shelter.

Luckily, figuring out how to get outside turned out to be pretty easy. After all, the window on the back door had been shattered when the Mitchells broke in. And since our Dad couldn't get anyone to fix it until after Christmas, he'd just taped a thick piece of plastic into place.

A thick piece of plastic that was pretty easy to push open if we jumped up hard enough.

Which was exactly what we did.

To begin, we gathered up all the toys we wanted to take and put them into one of our Mom's trash bags. The bag had long, tie handles that were perfect for our plan. Then Bogey jumped to the top of the window with the handles of the bag in his mouth. He pushed the plastic window cover out as he went, and landed on the ground outside. All the while, I stayed on the inside and pushed the bag up from below, while he pulled on the other side. Seconds later, we had that bag through the open window. Then I jumped up, went through the window opening, and landed outside, too.

A few minutes after that, we had the bag of toys loaded onto the wagon. Then I slipped into my harness while Bogey climbed aboard. I rolled the wagon down the driveway and past the front of our house. I said "Happy Birthday" to baby Jesus as I towed my wagon behind me.

Then I pulled it all the way to the cat shelter. Even though it was snowing just a little, I didn't mind. I was so excited about playing "Santa Claws" that the time seemed to fly by. I had to say, I really enjoyed all the gift-giving. Every time I gave something to someone else, I felt that Christmas spirit all over again.

Plus, I could hardly wait to see the happiness on the faces of the cats at the shelter. The idea of it gave me so much energy I could hardly contain myself.

"Hang on!" I yelled back to Bogey. "I'm going to make this wagon really move!"

"You got it, kid!" Bogey hollered back. "Let's see what this wagon can do!"

And then I took off at a run.

We arrived at the shelter just a few minutes later.

Holy Catnip!

Bogey and I knocked on the window.

"Let us in!" I yelled.

It's a little known fact that cats in the shelter let each other out of their cages at night. That's when they run around and play, and even work on the computer. Most shelter cats are really good with a computer by the time they get adopted into their forever homes.

So the whole bunch was up and running around, and they figured out a way to get us inside. A few minutes later, I was pulling my wagon into the shelter and we were handing out Christmas presents.

Well, let me tell you, it turned into quite a party. Treats were passed around and someone even found a little carton of milk that we shared. Everyone got a present, and the cats who didn't know about Christmas learned all about it.

You've never seen such a happy bunch of cats in your life.

Even so, one little black cat named Bella sat silently in the middle of the bunch. Her mouth drooped, and she didn't look like she was having fun at all.

I made my way over to her. "What's wrong? Aren't you enjoying the Christmas party?"

She shook her shiny head. "I'm sorry, Buckley. You've gone to a lot of work for us. And I sure appreciate all you've done."

Bogey came over and joined us.

I hunched down on the floor. "But something is bothering you."

She nodded. "All I want for Christmas is a forever home. Just like you have."

That's when Bogey and I looked at each other. Then we grinned.

"Remember what Mrs. Nelson said, kid?" Bogey asked me.

"That she wished she had a cat just like you? And me?" I answered him.

Bogey nodded at our wagon. "You got it, kid. I think we should give them a nice Christmas present, too."

I turned back to Bella. "I think we can help you get your Christmas wish."

Her gold eyes went wide. "You can?"

"You bet," Bogey answered.

A few minutes later, I was pulling our wagon back home. But this time Bogey and Bella were both in the back. We paused in front of our house just long enough to borrow some of the straw from baby Jesus' manger.

Then I rolled the wagon on over to the Nelsons' house. I pulled and Bogey pushed, and together, we managed to get it up on the front porch. We put the straw on the floor mat in front of the door and told Bella to lie on top. We'd already grabbed a bow from the shelter, so we put that on her head. It looked kind of like a hat.

"Are you ready?" I asked her.

She nodded her head and smiled. "Ready. Do you think they'll like me?"

"Are you kidding?" I asked. "They're gonna love you!"

Bogey rolled the wagon over so it was right below the doorbell. "Okay, kid. Climb in and reach up! Let's hope you're tall enough to pull this off!"

I hoped I was tall enough, too. But it turned out I had nothing to worry about at all. I got into the wagon and reached up until I could press the doorbell. I hit it twice, and then three more times in a row.

"That should be enough to wake up the Nelsons," I said as I climbed down.

"Okay, kid," Bogey told me. "Let's scram!"

"Good luck and Merry Christmas!" I told Bella as Bogey and I got our wagon off the porch.

"You, too, guys!" Bella said with a nervous smile. "Thanks so much for all your help."

"See you around the neighborhood," Bogey meowed as we pulled our wagon behind the shrubs.

And not a moment too soon.

The Nelsons swung the door open wide.

"What is it?" said Mr. Nelson in a sleepy voice. "What's wrong? Is there a problem?"

Then we heard Mrs. Nelson gasp. "Oh my goodness! Look. It's a miracle. A gift from Santa!"

I peeked out from behind the bushes to see Mrs. Nelson pick up Bella and hold her tight. Bella immediately began to purr.

"It looks like we have a new addition to our family," Mrs. Nelson said.

Mr. Nelson laughed. "I guess we do. But how did she get here?"

"It's probably one of those things we'll never understand," Mrs. Nelson said.

I caught a glimpse of Bella's face as Mrs. Nelson took her in and Mr. Nelson shut the door. It was a look of pure joy. For Bella had found a home.

After that, Bogey and I laughed and pranced all the way back to our home. We parked the wagon in the bushes and got back in the house the same way we'd gotten out.

Then we made a beeline for our Christmas tree. I could hardly believe my eyes. There were new cat toys and presents all over the place.

Holy Catnip! That sure was a lot of toys!

Lil sat relaxing in a chair, beside an empty glass of milk.

"What happened?" I breathed.

"It was Santa," said Lil. "You just missed him."

The Princess popped out from behind a bunch of presents. "He said you'd been so good this year, Buckley, that he brought you extra presents."

"He did?" I barely managed to ask.

Then all of a sudden the room felt like it was spinning. It was funny how things worked out. Here I'd given away most of my toys to cats who didn't have anything. And then I'd ended up with more toys than I ever had before.

I flopped over on my side. "I'm sorry we missed Santa," I said to Bogey.

But Bogey just grinned at me. "Don't sweat it, kid. There's always next year."

I was just starting to get my bearings again when I saw a sight I never thought I'd see.

The Wise One. Coming down the stairs.

She took each step slowly, carefully. Her legs were tottery, and she had to stop and get her balance again with each step.

The Princess rushed up to walk down with her.

But Bogey and Lil and I just sat there with our mouths hanging open. I could hardly believe what I was seeing.

Clearly this was a night for miracles.

Five minutes later, Miss Mokie and the Princess joined us all around the Christmas tree. Bogey and Lil and I bowed and then looked up at her again.

The Wise One sat as tall as she could and waved a paw above us. "I spoke with Santa before he departed," she announced. "He sends his regards, young Detectives. And Buckley, he hopes to meet you next year."

I just smiled in return. I hoped to meet him, too.

Then we all turned to gaze at the Christmas tree. It was such a beautiful sight. The lights twinkled and bounced off the shiny ornaments. The star at the top stood proudly, sparkling over it all.

"Merry Christmas," I said.

"Merry Christmas," the Princess chimed in.

Soon we were all saying it to each other.

When we were finished, I couldn't stop grinning. Sitting there with those cats on Christmas was one of the happiest moments I'd ever had.

When Bogey had told me Christmas was the best, well, he wasn't kidding.

Holy Catnip.

And Merry Christmas.

About the Author

Cindy Vincent was born in Calgary, Alberta, Canada, and has lived all around the US and Canada. She is the creator of the Mysteries by Vincent murder mystery party games and the Daisy Diamond Detective Series games for girls. She is also the award-winning author of the Buckley and Bogey Cat Detective Caper books, and the Daisy Diamond Detective book series. She lives with her husband and an assortment of fantastic felines.